Stepping Stones

A COLLECTION OF SHORT STORIES BY
MIRIAM R. KOSMAN

Stepping Stones

a collection of short stories by
MIRIAM R. KOSMAN

Copyright © 1992

All rights reserved.
This book, or any part thereof,
may not be reproduced in any
form whatsoever without the express
written permission of the copyright holder.

Published and distributed
in the U.S., Canada and overseas by
C.I.S. Publishers and Distributors
180 Park Avenue, Lakewood, New Jersey 08701
(908) 905-3000 Fax: (908) 367-6666

Distributed in Israel by
C.I.S. International (Israel)
Rechov Mishkalov 18
Har Nof, Jerusalem
Tel: 02-518-935

Distributed in the U.K. and Europe by
C.I.S. International (U.K.)
89 Craven Park Road
London N15 6AH, England
Tel: 81-809-3723

Book and cover design: Deenee Cohen
Typography: Nechamie Miller
Book and cover illustrations: Charlie Stern

ISBN 1-56062-141-9 hard cover
1-56062-142-7 soft cover

PRINTED IN THE UNITED STATES OF AMERICA

To my parents

Rabbi and Mrs. Moshe Eisemann

who through their personal example
always encouraged us
to look beyond the superficial.

Table of Contents

The Counselor's Twin 13

Free As a Bird 27

Just One Week 41

Pride Means Not Having to Hide 53

One of the Gang 67

Strawberry Ice Cream 79

Growing Pains 89

Training a Porcupine 101

A Sparrow's Song 127

The Counselor's Twin

The Counselor's Twin

I COULD SEE MY BROTHER STANDING AT THE CAMP gate as the bus swung into the driveway. Ari wasn't waving—that would have been beneath his dignity—but he was smiling his famous smile.

Well, you even merited a welcome at the gate, I told myself. The cynical thought tugged at my mind, making my spirits plummet even lower. I had been so glad to get away from the city for a few days that when Ari called up and suggested I visit him at camp I temporarily forgot that being with Ari was not really my idea of fun.

Not that it was Ari's fault. No one could accuse him of failing to display brotherly love. Actually, he was at his magnanimous best right now, ushering me around camp, arm slung around my shoulder, introducing me to everyone in sight.

That was the worst part. Watching eyebrows go up and seeing people search for something polite to say. You see, Ari and I are twins. It is hard for people to believe, because somehow, although many of our features are similar, the total pictures are very different.

Ari is tall, strong and good-looking. He has curly black hair, straight white teeth and a look of confidence about him. He is the type of boy that people smile at on the street. He is like a walking advertisement for a *yeshivah* day school, with his wholesome and honest appearance.

I, on the other hand, am a funny looking, skinny little guy with thick glasses and a mouth full of crooked teeth. I am about a head shorter than Ari. Even though I have the same curly black hair, it always manages to stick up all over my head in funny looking cowlicks, no matter how short the barber cuts it.

No wonder people were at a loss for words when Ari introduced me as his twin brother. As usual, Ari was totally unaware of my discomfort, although I felt like sinking into the ground. It was a relief to finally reach Ari's bunk, which was empty because all the campers had gone swimming. As a junior counselor, Ari was free until his campers came back from swimming.

As soon as I put my bag down next to the bed, another junior counselor burst into the bunk and asked Ari to come play baseball. Ari shot me a pleading look. I knew what

THE COUNSELOR'S TWIN

was going through his head. He hated to miss this baseball game, but he was torn between being a good host to me and going to play. He knew I would never join the game.

Always good at playing the martyr, I smiled cheerfully at Ari and his friend and said, "Go ahead, Ari. I want to rest anyway."

"Yeah, that was a long trip," Ari said while bustling around and arranging my bed. I could see that he was delighted at the chance to escape while still playing the part of a good host.

After Ari left, I stretched out on the bed, trying not to feel resentful. He was really such a nice guy—why couldn't I just accept him? Honestly, I told myself, is it his fault that he is great at sports and that you are the world's biggest *klutz*? You know he'd be happy to include you if you would show the slightest interest.

Deep down inside me, though, I knew I was just plain jealous. My parents never stopped trying to reassure me that I had my own talents, that I was better at school work, had more imagination, was good with little kids and so on. I had heard the list so often, I knew it by heart. Still, I was always convinced that Ari was the lucky one.

I squeezed my eyes shut trying to wipe out the picture that suddenly rose to my mind. I was remembering the day the camp director had come to our *yeshivah* to interview boys for the position of junior counselor. Of course, everyone in my class had applied, and of course, Ari was accepted before he had even had a chance to open his mouth. Ari's charming smile, and a glowing report from

STEPPING STONES

the principal, had the camp director hooked.

Naturally, I didn't stand a chance. Who would want a junior counselor who couldn't hold a baseball for three seconds without having it slip through his hands like wet spaghetti? My parents' litany of my pluses was useless this time, because it seemed that even the camp director wasn't interested in my talents with little children.

That night at supper, I could tell that everyone was trying to be extra nice, but my parents were exchanging worried looks. My mother kept making cheerful remarks about how she was so glad I would be home this summer, how I could take my younger sisters to the zoo and the library for her and other comments of this sort.

Even Ari was feeling a little guilty and decided he had to chime in. "Yeah, Yossi, you'll come and visit me for a week, and the rest of the time you can relax. You won't have a bunk full of kids on your head."

His condescending attitude was more than I could take. I put down my knife and fork, and in the iciest tone I could manage, I said, "You can keep your sympathy to yourself, Ari. I had no intention of going to that camp even if they had accepted me. I can think of better ways to spend my summer than up there in that boring camp!"

I knew no one was really fooled, but at least I was able to continue swallowing my food past the lump in my throat. My father quickly changed the subject.

And now here I was. After three weeks of *shlepping* my sisters to the zoo and the library in the sweltering heat, I no longer felt too proud to accept Ari's invitation. After this

THE COUNSELOR'S TWIN

morning's experiences, however, I was beginning to think that visiting camp was a mistake after all.

I walked to the door of the bunk and looked out. I could see the baseball field some distance to the left. Ari must have just hit a home run or something, because everyone was cheering and slapping him on the back.

Just then, someone called out his name. Looking to the right, I could see a crowd of boys carrying wet towels straggling up the hill. That must be his bunk coming back from swimming, I thought. Even from as far away as I stood, I could see Ari's reluctance as he threw down his bat and went to join them.

By the time Ari's campers had arrived at the bunk, he had managed to find his smile. He even introduced the kids to me quite cheerfully. As the kids went in to the washroom to change, though, he muttered to me, "I wish I could go back out there and finish the game with the other guys. They all have off this afternoon, but I've got to sit here and babysit during rest hour."

I had been wondering how Ari managed with these kids during the non-athletic activities. He would have no trouble teaching them to throw a fastball, but I couldn't imagine him entertaining them during rest hour.

On the other hand, the kids looked pretty cute to me. One in particular caught my eye. He reminded me of a chipmunk with his eager little face and his two front buck teeth.

Almost before I realized what I was doing, I said, "Ari, you go out and play ball. I'll entertain them for you today."

STEPPING STONES

Ari gave me a look of pure gratitude. "Would you really, Yossi? Thank you so much! Just be tough with them. They are a wild bunch!"

Before I could even ask him just what I was supposed to do, he had picked up his glove and left. I guess he was afraid I would change my mind if he stuck around too long.

The kids came shuffling back out of the washroom, looking at me kind of shyly. I racked my brain trying to think of what I could do with them to keep them busy, because I knew they wouldn't stay shy for very long. If I didn't occupy them soon, they would probably start having a pillow fight or something.

"Listen, kids," I said in my toughest voice, which to my chagrin came out like the bleat of a forlorn sheep. "I want you all sitting down on your beds. I am going to tell you a story."

"A story?" my chipmunk friend hooted. "We want to have a water fight!"

I gulped. A water fight was even worse than a pillow fight! Where was Ari? Why had I ever agreed to this? Fighting down my panic, I reminded myself that these were just little kids. Why, some of them looked about the size of my little sister. I could feel my courage returning. One thing I knew I could do was tell a good story. Before anyone had a chance to interrupt, I began, "Once upon a time, many, many years ago . . ."

The boys still stood around, uncertain whether to give in or not. I could see that, despite themselves, they were

THE COUNSELOR'S TWIN

interested. I ignored the ones still standing around near the washroom and focused on two boys sitting on their beds. I mustered up all of my storytelling abilities. Out of the corner of my eye, I could see the other boys edging closer and closer to the beds.

Twenty minutes later, they were all sitting there, completely spellbound. If I hadn't been at a sad point in the story, I would have laughed out loud. There sat all these wild little kids, completely mesmerized. I loved the way their eyes were glued to me, their faces mirroring every nuance of my story. I even noticed a tear glistening in the chipmunk kid's eyes.

Suddenly, my attention was caught by a movement on the porch. Someone was out there listening. I moved my chair back a little so that I could see who it was. To my surprise, I recognized the camp director. As soon as he saw I had noticed him, he disappeared as silently as he had come.

Instantly, my high spirits plummeted. I could just imagine what the director was thinking. Here was the boy that he had rejected as junior counselor, babysitting his brother's campers while his brother was out having a great time playing baseball. I had probably confirmed his image of me as Mr. Nebach.

I glanced down at my watch. Rest hour would be over in five minutes. I was going to finish this story, and then I'd call Ari. Wasn't he the one who was supposed to be their counselor? What did I need this for anyway? For the tenth time that day, I wished I was still back in the city. I

STEPPING STONES

would rather be stuck in sweltering heat than pitied. Too bad I was stuck here for the rest of the week.

The rest of the day dragged on wearily. I sat out on the sidelines during kickball and punchball, trying to look like I was enjoying the scenery. It wasn't until after supper that something really surprising happened.

I was just digging into a bowl of chocolate pudding (the first edible thing on the table that night) when a boy tapped me on the shoulder. I was informed that the camp director wanted to see me in his office.

My heart started pounding furiously. What could the camp director want from me? Had Ari forgotten to ask permission for me to come? Was he angry with me for taking over Ari's bunk during rest hour?

I was hoping Ari was around to help, but he was on the opposite side of the dining room, trying to finagle a few more portions of chocolate pudding. I had no choice but to follow the boy to the director's office.

The director called me in and asked me to sit down. I was expecting to be reprimanded, but what occurred was quite a surprise.

"I was standing outside the bunk and heard that story you were telling the kids," he said. "I was very impressed! You know, I have a problem with the current junior counselors. Although they're all good at sports, none of them know how to deal with the kids during quiet times."

Then he leaned back in his chair and really shocked me by saying, "I'd like to offer you the job of junior counselor, to take the place of one who just left. You'd also have to tell

THE COUNSELOR'S TWIN

a story every night during supper," he added.

I was absolutely ecstatic! After stammering my acceptance and thanks, I flew back to Ari's bunk to tell him the news.

The kids were out at a night activity, and Ari was busy straightening up the bunk. The minute I walked into the bunk, I blurted out my exciting news. I was sure he'd be thrilled at my success and relieved that he no longer needed to feel guilty about my not having been accepted.

Ari threw the towel he was holding across the room and dropped onto his bed. "That is great, Yossi," he muttered. "But the director is going to have to look for another new junior counselor, because I am leaving tomorrow."

"What?" I asked. "Why would you leave tomorrow?"

Ari kicked off his shoes and rolled over. "I knew I should never have invited you up here," he said, half to himself. "Figures that you would show up and ruin everything like you always do!"

"What are you talking about, Ari?" I sat down on the bed next to him and stared at him in disbelief. "When do I ever ruin things for you?"

"Boy, is this typical!" Ari went on, ignoring my question. "Here you come up to camp, where everyone thinks I am a great counselor, and now you are going to win all their hearts like you always do."

I was so shocked that I was at a loss for words. Ari wasn't waiting for my reply anyway.

"That's the way it's always been," he continued. "Even

the camp director was taken in by you."

I finally managed to find my voice. "Ari, what on earth are you talking about? You are the Mr. Popular that everyone loves. You know you are!"

"That's only until they meet you!" Ari said. "You know how our teachers all love you. They think you are so sweet and gentle and that I'm this big, noisy kid with a loud mouth. And Abba and Imma think you are wonderful. That's why they always take your side. You saw how glad they were to have you to themselves this summer. They were probably delighted that I was leaving for camp. And so was I! I was so glad to get away from you and the constant comparisons."

Ari sat up with a gesture of disgust. "I must have been crazy to invite you up here."

"But, Ari," I said, barely able to believe my ears. "You are the one that everyone loves. Why do you think the camp director chose you to be junior counselor? You are the one that always gets chosen first for all the teams. You are the handsome one. You know that everyone loves you!"

"Not once they meet you," Ari shot back. "Then they are always so touched by your sweet little face."

Suddenly, it hit me! This was the way things looked to Ari. I was amazed. Here I had been jealous of him for so many years, when all that time he had been just as jealous of me!

I looked at Ari. He was staring straight back at me as if he had never seen me before.

THE COUNSELOR'S TWIN

"Do you mean that all this time you thought . . ." he began.

"Did you really think . . ." I started at the same time.

We both burst out laughing. We collapsed on the floor, howling uncontrollably for minutes on end. I didn't even know what was so funny. It just felt so good to release all that tension. I felt like a dam inside me had burst.

Finally, Ari struggled to his feet, his face still red from laughter. "Well, after thirteen years, it's about time we got to know each other," he said. "Come on, Yossi," he reached down and gave me a hand. "Let's go talk to the director. Maybe with a little switching around, he can make you j.c. of my co-bunk."

And my twin brother and I strolled along to the office, arm in arm in the cool night air.

Free As a Bird

Free As a Bird

LEAH GLANCED CASUALLY AROUND HER BEDROOM AS she swung her sweater over her shoulder. She loved the way the bedspread fell in neat, crisp folds, the way her pencils and pencils lay neatly arranged on her desk. She smiled wryly as she thought how little her bedroom reflected her inner self. Nothing, it seemed, was neat and crisp in her life anymore. Nothing was the way it had been before the accident.

Leah closed the door of her bedroom and hurried down the stairs. She caught sight of herself in the hall mirror as she passed, and she grimaced. She knew she didn't look any different than she had before the accident. Her hair

STEPPING STONES

was still smooth and shining, the blue skirt of her school uniform still sharply pleated, her notes still written in a clear, round hand. It was only inside that she had changed. Inside, she felt jumbled, out of sorts, on edge.

The cool, clear air hit her with a refreshing blast as she opened the front door. Leah breathed deeply as she hurried along. Maybe if she just acted as if she was the same old capable, level-headed, unruffled Leah, things would eventually click back into place.

But as she passed the street corner, "the scene of the accident," as they called it in the papers, she knew that things would never be the same again. For a moment, her mind was full of the memory of that day—she and Sarit Lopel stepping off the curb together, carrying the big puppet theater that almost blocked their vision, the sudden screech of brakes, Sarit's scream, then the blackness.

Leah quickly tossed her head, trying to clear her mind of the flood of memories. She didn't want to think about the long months she had spent recovering from a broken leg, and she certainly didn't want to think about that gray, bleak day when she had found out that, while her own broken leg would soon heal, Sarit would be crippled forever.

As she turned into Sarit's street, she could feel the blanket of guilt descending on her again, almost smothering her. The words pounded in her brain, as they did every day, increasing in tempo with her hurrying footsteps. Why Sarit? she thought. Why does Sarit have to go through life as a cripple? And the thought that hid behind those

FREE AS A BIRD

words repeated itself. Why did I escape scot-free?

A leaf falling from the tree above floated gently down to graze Leah's cheek and pulled her away from her thoughts. She squared her shoulders and looked up at the clear, blue sky. She would never know the answer to her question, but one thing was certain. Leah would make sure that, as long as she was around, Sarit would lack for nothing. She would never allow Sarit to be alone, a pitiful cripple. She was determined to stand by her side, protecting her, helping her and shielding her from curious and prying eyes.

Leah hurried up the front steps to Sarit's house, clearing two bicycles and a toy car out of her way as she went. It seemed that her life would forever be divided into two stages—before the accident and after the accident. She had always loved the chaotic cheerfulness of the Lopel home, which was so different from her own orderly, only-child existence. But now it seemed, that although the chaos was still there, some of the cheerfulness was gone. It seemed that Sarit's condition had managed to dampen even the free-flying spirits of the Lopel family.

"Hi, Leah," Mrs. Lopel's voice emerged from the darkness behind the screen door. "Come on in. The gang is gone already, so you can sit down and have some cookies and milk until Sarit is ready."

Leah followed her nose into the kitchen, sniffing appreciatively. "Boy, Mrs. Lopel, freshly baked chocolate chip cookies on a Monday morning! I hope Sarit is late more often!"

STEPPING STONES

Mrs. Lopel laughed as she picked up the baby and carried her over to the sink to wash her face. "Well, Leah," she said, "you certainly deserve any treats we can give you!"

Leah had the feeling that she and Mrs. Lopel had an unspoken agreement to speak extra loudly to each other when they heard Sarit coming, almost as if they were trying to drown out the silence and the sound of Sarit shuffling slowly down the hallway.

Leah couldn't help remembering the other Sarit. The pre-accident Sarit who used to come flying down the hallway on her skateboard, a little brother under each arm, singing *Oh, What a Beautiful Morning* at the top of her lungs.

Leah stood up abruptly in an attempt to change the mood. "Ready to go, Sarit?" she asked.

"Leah," Mrs. Lopel said, turning suddenly from the sink. "Sit down. I want to talk to you about something. It will only take a minute."

Leah stiffened and glanced quickly at Sarit's face for a clue as to what this might be about, but Sarit's face was blank as she looked curiously at her mother. Leah's stomach began to churn. Maybe Mrs. Lopel had heard about how she had gone roller skating last Sunday afternoon with Shiffy instead of coming over to the Lopels as she usually did.

"What do you think about Sarit starting her puppet shows again, Leah?" Mrs. Lopel asked, looking straight at Leah.

FREE AS A BIRD

Leah sat down again with a gasp. Whatever she had been expecting, it certainly wasn't a suggestion like this.

"What? How?" she sputtered, not knowing how to respond.

"It's really very simple, Leah," Mrs. Lopel continued calmly. "It's been over a year since the accident, and Sarit's father and I feel it is about time Sarit got on with her life. She can't hang on to you forever, and there is really no reason why she shouldn't do puppet shows."

"No reason why she shouldn't?" Leah almost shouted. "Mrs. Lopel, do you really want her standing up there with everyone staring at her, pitying her?"

Leah glanced quickly at Sarit, wondering whether she should go on. But Sarit was still sitting there, docilely eating her cookies, almost as if the conversation was about someone else entirely.

In a sense, it really was about someone else, Leah realized suddenly. This docile, compliant, almost lifeless girl bore no resemblance to the old Sarit. Sarit the puppeteer. Sarit the fireball, full of ideas and excitement. Sarit, who had always been on the run, with Leah breathlessly at her heels. This quiet girl who clung to Leah's arm like a heavy bracelet was a different person. Now it was even possible to talk about her with her own mother, while she was still in the room, without her commenting. It was as if her sparkle had been snuffed out together with the use of her right hand and leg.

"I really don't think you are right," Mrs. Lopel said, bringing Leah back to the present. "I think that once Sarit

STEPPING STONES

begins her puppet show, everyone will be so interested that they will forget to stare at her. And I think you could also use a break anyway. You have probably been neglecting your own interests."

For a moment, Leah felt a flicker of hope stirring inside her. She was sure no one had guessed how much she yearned to be back out on the field playing *machanayim* and kickball. That stolen Sunday afternoon on the roller skating rink had been a tonic for her, and if Mrs. Lopel thought that it would be good for Sarit also . . . The thought of escape was so tempting.

But no, Leah commanded herself firmly. You made a promise not to leave Sarit to fend for herself, not to leave her to a fate that could just have easily been yours. Your job is to stick by her side and protect her, and that is what you are going to do.

Aloud, she said, "Mrs. Lopel, Sarit and I enjoy being together. Also, I am sure that Sarit has no desire to stand up there and have everyone applaud her and pretend the puppet show is terrific just because they feel sorry for her."

Suddenly, Sarit's head shot up. "For your information, Leah dear, the accident did not affect my brain or my ability to perform. There is no reason that they wouldn't enjoy one of my original puppet shows!"

Mrs. Lopel clapped her hands. "Thatta' girl, Sarit!" she said.

Leah looked at Sarit's defiant face in surprise. So there was still some life in her.

But the next minute, the invisible curtain fell over

FREE AS A BIRD

Sarit's face again, and she turned to her mother and said in a tired voice, "Don't get your hopes up, Imma. I'm not going to do a puppet show anyway. I have enough trouble getting around, keeping up with my school work and writing with my left hand. Anyway, the truth is that the girls do look at me differently now."

"But that's because you don't give them a chance to see that the real you hasn't changed . . ." Mrs. Lopel began.

Sarit stood up. "Forget it, Imma," she said, and then turning to Leah, "Let's go."

Mrs. Lopel accompanied them to the door, looking totally undisturbed by Sarit's outburst. Leah guessed that she was probably delighted at the flicker of Sarit's old fire.

"Okay, girls," Mrs. Lopel said as she swung the big front door open for them. "We'll close the discussion for now." She winked at Sarit mischievously. "But Leah, I hope you didn't misunderstand me. We think you are the most wonderful friend that Sarit could have. Now have a wonderful day, girls!" She pulled Leah close to her in a swift hug and whispered in her ear, "Always remember that the biggest gift you can ever give someone is independence."

And the big front door swung shut.

"Now what was that supposed to mean?" Leah muttered half to herself and half to Sarit. She was feeling thoroughly confused. She would love for Sarit to be independent. Did Mrs. Lopel think she enjoyed having two lives to lead? If Sarit would be able to manage on her own, and if she could be sure that people wouldn't smother her

STEPPING STONES

with pity, Leah would have let her go long ago.

But the trouble is that I can't, Leah's thoughts rumbled on. I can't just abandon her to her fate. Somehow I still feel like I owe her something because I escaped unharmed while she has all the suffering.

Suddenly, Leah realized that she was very tired. Her throat even felt scratchy. Maybe she was coming down with something. What a relief that would be, to be able to collapse into bed for a few days and forget all about the Lopel family. If they are so anxious for Sarit to be independent, let them see how she gets along without me for a few days, Leah thought defiantly. Then maybe they will appreciate me!

As soon as she deposited Sarit in the classroom, Leah went straight to the school nurse to see whether she could be sent home. The nurse took one look at Leah's troubled face and needed little convincing. Leah soon found herself safely tucked in bed with a box of tissues, a thermos of hot tea and her mother's comforting prescription of three days of rest.

What a relief! Leah let herself drift off into a drowsy warm sleep, where she could forget all about Sarit and puppet shows and independence and accidents.

It took more than three days to recover from what turned out to be strep throat. It wasn't until the following Tuesday morning, which turned out to be *Rosh Chodesh*, that Leah was allowed to leave the house. She hurried along to Sarit's house feeling slightly guilty and worried about what Sarit would say about all the "urgent" phone

FREE AS A BIRD

messages Leah had ignored. The episode at Sarit's house of the previous week seemed far in the past, and Leah was not looking forward to getting involved again.

Mrs. Lopel met Leah at the door with a strange look on her face. "Sarit's gone on ahead, Leah. She wasn't sure if you'd be better, so Shiffy and Rachel picked her up today."

A sense of foreboding suddenly tightened Leah's stomach. She glanced up at the overcast sky warily and hurried along to school.

It wasn't until she arrived at the school building that her worst fears came true. Leah stared in shock at the sign on the big bulletin board in the front hall.

"SARIT LOPEL AND HER PUPPETS ARE BACK!" the sign proclaimed in huge letters. "IN HONOR OF *ROSH CHODESH*, SARIT AND HER MERRY PUPPETS WILL BE PERFORMING TODAY IN THE AUDITORIUM AT TWO O'CLOCK."

Leah felt as if she had been punched in the stomach. So they had gone ahead with it after all!

The sound of laughter echoing down the hall caught Leah's attention. It seemed so familiar and yet so strange. In a second, she recognized the source. Sarit was sitting on the stairs, surrounded by a crowd of girls. Leah's heart jumped, and for a moment, she closed her eyes. Maybe this whole last year had just been a horrible dream and she was just waking up now.

But no! As she watched from her hidden spot around the corner, the whole crowd of laughing and chatting girls moved off down the hallway, and she could see Sarit limping along, slightly behind all of them, except for

STEPPING STONES

Shiffy who was walking with her. A pang of sympathy for Sarit shot through Leah so sharply that she had to remind herself that it wasn't physical. How she wished that she could somehow make Sarit "normal" again like all the other girls!

Leah spent the rest of the morning alternating between rage and concern. How on earth would Sarit manage to pull the puppet strings all by herself? she wondered. And the next minute, She's crazy! What is she trying to prove?

Leah sat glowering fiercely through her first two classes. She didn't even glance in Sarit's direction, although she noticed Sarit trying to catch her attention. Later, sitting alone and lonely in the back of the auditorium, even the sight of Sarit struggling awkwardly up the aisle, carrying her puppet bag on her one good arm, did not soften Leah's heart. If Sarit wants to be so independent and thinks she can manage without my help, then let her just try, she thought.

As soon as the curtain opened, Leah forgot to feel angry and hurt. In fact, she forgot to feel anything. She became completely lost in the show, as Sarit's clear, sweet, animated voice began weaving her story, taking on the tones of the different characters. If the puppets' movements were a little jerky, the drama of the story more than made up for that deficiency.

The main character was a little boy puppet with a colorful *yarmulka* on his head. His cheerful grin and bright blue eyes reminded Leah of Sarit's younger brother. Leah watched as the little boy sauntered across an open field

FREE AS A BIRD

and suddenly came across a bird with a broken wing. She listened to Sarit's voice tell how the boy took the bird home and put it in a cage, loving it and caring for it.

Leah watched, mesmerized, as the starving and frightened bird was slowly tamed and grew steadily stronger. Leah saw the bird begin beating its wings against the sides of the cage. Her heart thumped faster when Sarit's voice, talking as the little boy, told the audience that the bird's wing would never heal and that it needed to be clipped. She watched as the bird learned how to fly around the cage in its new and awkward way.

Leah found herself hanging on the edge of her seat, her hand gripping the chair in front of her, as the boy struggled to decide whether or not to let the bird fly free. She listened as he described in great detail all the dangers that awaited a bird who couldn't fly properly. The boy puppet then turned to look at the cage where the bird continuously beat its wings against the walls.

The whole audience, including Leah, breathed a sigh of relief as the boy slowly and dramatically opened the cage. The bird soared out, flexing its wings and resting briefly on the boy's shoulder, before winging its way, however clumsily, up into the clear blue sky of the puppet theater. Leah's eyes were filled with tears as the little boy puppet leaned against the window, gazing up into the sky and said, in Sarit's voice this time, "I guess love means letting my friend try his own wings."

The curtain fell, and Sarit stepped in front of the puppet theater. Leah had to catch her breath at the sight

STEPPING STONES

of Sarit standing there, her blue eyes glowing, her cheeks pink with excitement, her hair tousled, her face wreathed in smiles. When had she last seen Sarit looking like that?

And the standing ovation! The people standing next to her and around her, stamping their feet, clapping, with tears rolling down their cheeks. Nobody could call this pity! This was unbridled admiration—admiration for someone who had the courage to open the doors to her own cage and fly free.

Over the heads of the crowd, Leah caught Sarit's eye. She stood still for a moment recalling the hurt of the last months. Then she let her folding chair clatter back as she walked over to envelop Sarit in a giant bear hug, cutting the last wires of her own cage.

Just One Week

Just One Week

TZIPPI REACHED UP TO THE SECOND SHELF TO HANG the cups on their hooks. She folded the blue dish towel over the bar and thought about how to tell her mother what was bothering her.

It was very quiet in the house. All the children were sleeping. Abba was out teaching a class. This was the best time to talk to Imma undisturbed, but Tzippi couldn't think of how to start.

Imma finally broke the silence.

"So what did the class decide to do for its *chessed* project?"

Tzippi put away the dish rack under the sink. "They

STEPPING STONES

didn't decide yet. There is supposed to be a meeting about it on Monday."

"Any ideas?" Imma pushed her needle through the button one last time and tied a knot.

"One thing is for sure, whatever they do, it won't include me!" Tzippi angrily threw her sponge on the counter. This was exactly what she wanted to talk to Imma about.

"It must be hard to live so far away from the rest of your class." Imma's voice was understanding. "I guess you feel pretty isolated."

"You said it!" Tzippi squeezed the sponge out and turned to face Imma. She watched Imma pull Simchah's shirt out of the mending basket. "I'm really sick of it, Imma. All the girls talk about is what they are going to do after school, who will visit whom on *Shabbos* afternoon or where they'll go on Sunday. Mrs. Becker said that this *chessed* project is supposed to unify the class. You know, they'll spend Sunday afternoon all together doing something worthwhile. Well, I can tell you, one person it won't unify—me!" Tzippi stooped to pick up a spool of thread. "How is a person supposed to make friends when they live fifty miles away from everyone else? That's something I want to know!"

"You know you can always invite your friends here for *Shabbos*," Imma said quietly.

"It's not the same, Imma." Tzippi flipped the spool impatiently. "How often could they come, anyway?"

"Well, I guess we could drive you down some Sundays

JUST ONE WEEK

to join in this *chessed* project, if it's so important to you," Imma said thoughtfully.

"Oh, Imma. I'd never want that. Sunday is *Abba's* one day free from driving me. I'll . . . I'll figure something out."

Tzippi wished she'd never brought up the subject. The last thing she wanted was to make Imma feel bad.

"What do you think they'll do for this project, anyway?" Imma asked, changing the subject.

"Oh, the usual. They'll probably have a clothes drive or put on a play to raise money for *tzeddakah*. Whatever they discuss, they'll end up doing what Rachel Shiffer wants anyway. They always do what she says, and her mother is in charge of sending clothes packages to Israel."

She paused for a minute, forgetting that she wouldn't be a part of it. "I wish there was something real we could do. Something that would make a difference to someone."

"Like what?" Imma asked.

"Like . . . like visiting a hospital and getting to know the patients or . . . or. . . Imma, the Sinai Old Age Home!"

Tzippi jumped off her chair excitedly. "Imma, the home is right off our exit. Abba always says that it's the worst place to have a Jewish old age home because it's so far from any Jews."

Imma smiled, catching Tzippi's enthusiasm. "What are you thinking?"

"We could go there every Sunday. The girls can arrange car pools. Every parent would have to drive only two or three times a year." Tzippi ran over to the drawer and pulled out a pad and pen.

STEPPING STONES

"We could perform songs and skits and afterwards just walk around and talk to the people." She licked the top of the pen and positioned it over the paper thoughtfully. "What do you think, Imma?"

"It sounds like a wonderful idea, Tzippi. Maybe the girls could come over here afterwards for some refreshments."

Tzippi grinned at her mother. "Well, so much for the idea. Now, I have to see if I can make it work!"

An hour later, Tzippi had filled up three pages with plans. On top of her list was to call the old age home and make an appointment to discuss her idea with the entertainment coordinator. She also had to work out a car pool plan and a tentative schedule for the first week.

It was ten o'clock by the time she went up to bed, her head whirling with ideas. As she walked upstairs, she suddenly had a terrible thought.

"Imma, what if they don't like the idea?"

She could hear the smile in Imma's voice as she said, "Tzippi! You try your best. Leave the rest up to Hashem! Now, good night."

The next Sunday morning, Abba drove Tzippi to the old age home. Tzippi had an eleven o'clock appointment with Mrs. Carver, the entertainment coordinator.

Mrs. Carver met Tzippi at the door of her office.

"Come on in, and let's discuss your plan, dearie. You're just Heaven-sent, Heaven-sent, I say!"

Abba was waiting outside when Tzippi finished. She flew to the car and bounced into her seat.

JUST ONE WEEK

"Mrs. Carver was so glad, Abba," Tzippi burst out, her voice fairly bubbling. "She said the people would love to have some young Jewish girls visit them. She kept saying, 'You're Heaven-sent.'" Tzippi laughed at the memory. "I told her that I'd let her know by Wednesday if we were coming. She was so happy . . . oh, Abba!" Again, the frightening thought clutched Tzippi's stomach. "What if they don't want to come?"

School on Monday morning found Tzippi sitting in her seat in the second row, biting her nails. There were four suggestions up on the board, and the girls were arguing loudly. Tzippi waited until all the other girls had given their ideas. Then she raised her hand. Mrs. Becker asked her to come to the front of the room to present her idea. Tzippi could hear the surprise in Mrs. Becker's voice. She wasn't used to Tzippi joining in discussions about things that were done outside of school.

Tzippi walked to the front of the room. She looked around the classroom. All the girls were looking at her. They were also surprised to see her up there.

Tzippi opened her looseleaf, took out her sheet of plans, and began to speak. She told the girls what her Abba had said, about how lonely the old people were because they lived so far from the Jewish community. She told them how Mrs. Carver had said that the people rarely get visitors and how excited Mrs. Carver had been about her ideas. She described the car pool plan and told them of Imma's suggestion of having the class over for refreshments afterwards. The girls listened quietly while she was

STEPPING STONES

talking. Tzippi could feel their interest. No one else had presented their plan so thoroughly.

When she was finished, everyone started talking at once. Devorah said her mother would surely be able to drive this week. Gila said she had a great idea for a skit they could put on. Nechama said her great-aunt lived there and her mother would love for her to visit her.

Finally, Mrs. Becker stood up. She had a big smile on her face.

"Okay, girls, this is a new idea," she said. "We'll hear what each of you has to say, but one by one."

The girls stopped talking and began waving their hands frantically in the air.

Mrs. Becker called on Rachel.

"I think it's a dumb idea!" Rachel announced. "Who wants to *shlep* halfway across the world to do *chessed*? And anyway, what would we say to these old people? It will be so much easier just to collect clothes."

Everyone's eyes turned to Tzippi.

"It is not a dumb idea!" Tzippi retorted. "How would you like it if you were old and lonely and people didn't want to visit you because they had nothing to say? And anyway, the harder it is, the bigger the *mitzvah!*" Tzippi stopped for breath and thought of something else. "The whole idea of *chessed* is to get personally involved, anyway."

Devorah waved her hand directly into Mrs. Becker's face. She was almost falling out of her chair in her excitement.

JUST ONE WEEK

"I think it's a great idea! My mother will be able to drive for sure."

"I'm telling you," Nechama repeated, "my great-aunt lives there. My mother will really be thrilled if we all go visit her."

The room erupted into bedlam again, with each girl calling out her ideas.

Mrs. Becker stood up again. "All right, girls. I hear a lot of different opinions. We'll take a vote." She cleared the blackboard. "Who does not like the old age home idea?"

Rachel immediately raised her hand. Then she turned around and glared at Shaini and Chayalah. They slowly raised their hands, too. Chavie and Shulamis turned around to look at Rachel. They also raised their hands. Mrs. Becker marked five under opposed.

"Who's for it?"

The rest of the class raised their hands.

"Well, that settles it." Mrs. Becker erased the board. "Tzippi, I think it's a wonderful idea. Let's get some of those plans on the blackboard."

For the rest of the hour, the girls discussed car pool plans and ideas for their presentation at the old age home.

Devorah and Leah walked Tzippi out to her car that afternoon. They were still discussing Sunday's project.

"See you tomorrow," they called as the car swung down the driveway.

All week long, the girls practiced and planned. Tzippi ran from one group to the next, organizing, advising and helping.

47

STEPPING STONES

"Tzippi, do you think we should perform songs, do a dance or just a skit?"

"Tzippi, my mother is going to call your mother tonight to find out exact directions."

"Tzippi, we must work on that new song. Can you sleep over tomorrow night so we can practice?"

On Wednesday, Rachel came over to Tzippi.

"My mother thinks it's a great idea, Tzippi," she said. "My mother says I have to get involved."

Tzippi noticed the discomfort on Rachel's face.

This is a *chessed* project in more ways than one, Tzippi thought to herself and smiled inwardly.

"That's great, Rachel," she answered. "Why don't you teach us that new song your brother made up?"

It was Sunday afternoon. Tzippi looked around the big lounge. She was glowing with happiness. All the girls were scattered around talking to different people. She saw Devorah in the corner talking excitedly to a little old lady in a green robe. Saralah was helping another one cross the room to her chair.

Tzippi walked over to the hot water dispenser to make old Mrs. Levine some tea. Rachel was sitting next to the dispenser, talking to a sweet-looking old woman with glasses. Rachel was sitting on the edge of her chair and pulling at her braid nervously.

"This is so wonderful," the lady with the glasses said. "Whose idea was it?"

"Oh, I guess it was all of ours," Rachel answered in a

JUST ONE WEEK

"Oh, I guess it was all of ours," Rachel answered in a proud voice, looking relieved to have something to talk about.

Tzippi smiled to herself as she dipped the tea bag into the steaming water.

Late Sunday evening, Tzippi went down to the kitchen for a drink. Her friend Devorah was sleeping over and was upstairs waiting for her.

Tzippi filled two red cups with apple juice. Imma was standing at the sink, finishing up with the dishes.

"I can't believe it, Imma!" Tzippi said. "It went so perfectly. The old people loved it. I made friends with Mrs. Levine. I can't wait to see her next week. Mrs. Carver was so grateful!" Tzippi paused for a moment to get some cookies out of the cabinet. She arranged them on the plate. "Then, all the girls coming over here and Devorah sleeping over. In the end, even Rachel told me that it was a great idea. It seems like the whole world has changed in just one week!"

Pride Means Not Having to Hide

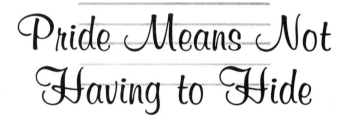

Pride Means Not Having to Hide

THE MAIN THING ABOUT CHANI AND ME IS THAT WE understand each other. We didn't always, though. In the beginning, I thought she was weird and she thought I was stuck up, cold and unfeeling. But that was before we met at the park that day. Well, maybe I had better start at the beginning.

It all started last September, on the first day of school. It was my first day in the seventh grade, but it was Chani's first day in our school. Her family had just moved to town, so for her it was really a big first.

I had always been a regular, average type of girl. You know, not excelling at anything in particular and not very

STEPPING STONES

poor at anything either. Or perhaps I should say, I was almost regular and average. Because, you see, I had a secret. My secret was Avramie, my younger brother.

Avramie was eight years old, but he acted like a four-year-old. He drooled a lot and couldn't talk clearly, but he was the happiest kid you ever saw.

Now don't get me wrong—I really love Avramie and I spent a lot of time with him at home. But school was another story altogether. My situation just wasn't the type of thing that you would expect other seventh-graders to understand. I mean, here they all were with siblings going to the same schools. And here I was, with Avramie as my only brother, going every day on a special bus to a special school. I just figured that the less said about it the better.

Of course, the girls who lived in my neighborhood saw Avramie every once in a while, but I never talked about him and I hoped they wouldn't either. It wasn't that I was ashamed. I just wanted to play it safe.

Well, that was until Chani came. It sure isn't a secret any more. Sometimes, it still bothers me that everyone knows, but mostly, I'm glad. That's also how we became such good friends. Like I said, it all started that first day of school.

The morning bell had already rung. Most of us were in our seats, talking with each other across the aisle, when the door suddenly flew open and in walked Chani. Usually, when someone is new at a school, they come in very shyly, choose a seat in the back of the room and busy themselves with their books, pretending not to notice the stares. I'm

PRIDE MEANS NOT HAVING TO HIDE

sure you've seen it often enough.

But not Chani! Chani bounced right into the classroom, her red curls flying, her glasses perched on the tip of her nose, and flopped right into a seat in the third row between two other girls. She turned around and flashed this big, bright smile at the rest of the girls in the class, who were all staring at her dumfounded.

"Hi, y'all," she said. "My name is Chani Lightner, and I'm from Memphis, Tennessee."

Then she turned to Rachel Felder and said, "Hey, weren't you at my cousin Sheila's wedding in June? I thought you looked familiar! Are you related to her husband?"

After she had finished charming Rachel, and discussing how wonderful her cousin was, she turned to Shifra and said, "We passed each other at the mall this week, when I was shopping with my mother, didn't we? Did you get those shoes you were looking at?"

By now, she had the whole class laughing and talking and asking her questions. Chani was lapping it up, nodding and smiling for all the world as if she were the Queen of Siam.

All this time, I was cringing in my seat, trying my very best to disappear. I dreaded Chani looking in my direction. I knew I would look familiar to her, too, and the problem was, I knew where I had seen her.

Avramie's school had started the day before, and since my mother had a dentist appointment, I was elected to stand outside with him and wait for his bus. When the bus

STEPPING STONES

finally pulled up, I saw this girl inside with her arm around a little boy who looked about the same size as Avramie. The girl seemed about my age. I remembered hearing my parents talking at the dinner table about a new family that had moved here from Memphis in order to send their son to Avramie's school, which was supposed to be a very good one. So, being the genius that I am, I just put two and two together and realized that Chani must be the new boy's sister and that she had been taking him to school. Now, what if she announced to the class where she had seen me?

Just then, Chani looked up, and her gaze fell right on me. She smiled her happy smile, and as I tried to drop lower into my seat she said, "Didn't I see you yesterday waiting for the special bus with a little boy? Is that your brother?"

I could feel my face turning bright red. Just then, the bell rang, and Rabbi Katz strode into the classroom, commanding everyone's attention and saving me from having to reply.

I felt so angry, I could barely concentrate on a word that Rabbi Katz was saying! Who did that girl think she was? Acting like she owned the world! What right did she have to discuss my business in public? Thoughts flew through my head like racing cars, making me angrier by the minute. Doesn't she have any delicacy? Doesn't she know when to keep her mouth shut?

Well, believe me, she wasn't finished yet. Not Chani! The minute the bell rang, signaling recess, she came

PRIDE MEANS NOT HAVING TO HIDE

marching down the aisle, right to my seat and started in again.

"Was that your little brother you put on the bus yesterday?" she asked. "What's your name by the way?"

I was so flustered that, as I pushed back my chair to get up, I managed to knock a whole pile of books and pencils off my desk. I bent down to pick up the books from the floor, and Chani kneeled down next to me.

"How old is he?" she asked. "He's really sweet!"

She was so busy asking questions that she didn't even notice that I hadn't answered one yet. I grabbed my new math book out of her hand.

"Will you stay out of my business?" I hissed. "Don't you know better than to ask me these questions in front of everyone?" I could feel my hands trembling in anger.

Chani sat back on her heels and stared at me. Her big, bright smile faded, and a red spot appeared on either cheek. Her eyes seemed to get bigger and rounder behind her glasses.

"Don't tell me that you are ashamed of him? Why, you stuck up, snobby . . ." Chani was literally sputtering. I'd never seen anyone so furious before. "You should be ashamed of yourself!" And with that, Chani stormed out of the room, leaving me with a queasy stomach and a pile of books and pencils to pick up with shaking hands.

Well, from that day on, Chani ignored me. She made lots of friends; everyone else loved her. She was invited to a different girl's house almost every day, but she never said a word to me.

STEPPING STONES

She talked a lot about her little brother Yossi. Sometimes, she told the girls who invited her over that she couldn't come because she was taking Yossi to the park. Once, she even brought in a picture of him. I caught a glimpse of it on Rachel Felder's desk. Chani and her two older brothers were grouped around a chair, and in the chair was Yossi, with his head lolling to one side, his arms all twisted up, and a big smile on his face. He reminded me of Avramie.

I could see that the girls didn't know exactly how to react. Rachel tried a tentative response. "He looks a little like your older brother."

Chani didn't even seem to notice how uncomfortable the others were. "Yes," she said with a laugh. "He has the famous Lightner nose, that's for sure."

I thought a lot about what was going on. Even though the girls seemed uncomfortable with the picture, no one seemed to be less friendly with Chani. She was still so popular. But I still wasn't going to risk mentioning Avramie. After all, I didn't have Chani's charming southern accent, red curls and blue eyes. I was sure that if I wasn't just like everybody else no one would ever be my friend.

Things would have continued this way, with Chani ignoring me and me being jealous of her popularity, if it hadn't been for a certain beautiful Sunday afternoon in the middle of November. It had been raining all week, and Avramie had to stay home with a cold. Then, all of a sudden, the sun came out, the sky cleared up, and it felt

PRIDE MEANS NOT HAVING TO HIDE

almost like spring. Of course, my mother got this gleam in her eye she always gets when she has an idea she knows I might not like too much.

"Dena, how would you like to take Avramie to the park today? He has been so cooped up all week and it's such a beautiful day . . ." she let her sentence trail off, looking at me hopefully.

Of course, that was the last thing I wanted to do, but before I knew it, there I was wheeling a bundled-up Avramie in his stroller down the street to the park.

And whom should I see, standing by the swings? You guessed it. It was Chani, red curls flying, pushing her little brother as high as he could go. Well, as you can imagine, the first thing I wanted to do was head in the opposite direction, which is what I did. But Avramie would have none of that. He had caught sight of Yossi on the swing, and he started waving his arms and yelling.

"Come on, Avramie," I said. "Don't you want to come feed the ducks?"

Avramie wasn't even listening. His whole body was wriggling, and he was stretching out his arms to Yossi and laughing. Yossi was reacting the same way. Chani let the swing slow down, and Yossi almost fell out of the front of it in his excitement over seeing Avramie!

Chani stopped the swing without looking at me and pulled Yossi out. She lugged him over to Avramie's stroller and put him on the grass in front of it. I leaned over and unstrapped Avramie and placed him on the grass next to Yossi. Then I threw a bright red ball that my mother had

STEPPING STONES

stuffed into our picnic bag. It landed on the grass in front of them.

Were those two kids happy! They kept rolling around in the grass, gripping the ball and then letting it roll away, giggling and laughing all the while.

They were having such a great time that I couldn't help smiling, too. I glanced shyly at Chani. She was also smiling. She caught my glance and looked away, confused. Just then, the ball slipped out of Yossi's hand and rolled down the incline.

"I'll get it," I called and raced after it.

I tossed it to Chani, who caught it with one hand and threw it back to Yossi. Yossi picked it up from the grass and let it slide towards Avramie. Avramie turned to me and tried to aim the ball in my direction. I couldn't believe my eyes. They were playing catch!

Chani and I laughed and played with our brothers for over an hour as if we were the best of friends. We swung them on the swings and let them slide down the sliding board, but it wasn't until we were giving them lunch that we really started to talk.

"I'm sorry I called you snobby," Chani said, looking down at the brown paper bag in her hand. "I guess I was just so hurt for your brother that I lost my temper."

I just stared at the banana I was holding and didn't answer. I didn't think I could trust my voice.

"You know, I discussed it with my parents later," Chani continued. "They explained to me that other people might not feel the same way we do about Yossi and that

PRIDE MEANS NOT HAVING TO HIDE

other people might not be comfortable with everyone knowing about their private lives."

"What do you mean?" I managed to ask.

"Well, when Yossi was born, it was a big shock. I mean I was only five at the time, but from what I've heard, all our relatives were very upset. Here, my parents had three beautiful children—if I do say so myself!" Chani flashed her famous smile. "And then Yossi was born. They knew right away that something was wrong. My parents sat down and had a long discussion to decide how they were going to deal with the situation.

"They felt that in a way, it was a compliment from Hashem that He had given them a child who needed special care and attention. It was as if Hashem was saying, 'I know you can do it.' They decided that they were going to do everything in their power to help Yossi grow and develop. They would never hide him away! They would expose him to all types of situations so that he would be more equipped to deal with life." Chani paused for breath. "I always got the feeling that my parents were very grateful for having been given a special child. My father always tells us that Yossi has a *heilege neshamah*, a holy soul, because he can never even think of doing anything wrong."

I was listening spellbound. Things were so different in my family, I wondered if I could make her understand.

"There are only the two of us in our family," I began hesitantly. "I was born after my parents were married many years, and they were very proud of me. When I was

61

STEPPING STONES

five, Avramie was born, and it seems like everything changed. My parents are always sitting up late at night and talking in whispers. Whenever I come in, they stop and smile at me, but I know they are talking about Avramie and what will be with him." I stopped for a minute to get up my courage. Chani might not like my next question. "Aren't you worried? Don't you worry about what will be with Yossi?"

I glanced quickly at Chani. She was crumpling up her paper bag into a hard ball.

"Of course, I worry," Chani answered in a quiet voice. "Sometimes, I can't even fall asleep at night thinking about what will be when we are all grown up. But my father says that is not our job. We don't have to worry about what will be. We have to do our *hishtadlus*; we have to make an effort. We have to try our best to make him as self-sufficient as possible, to strengthen his muscles, to teach him as much as he can learn—and we have to *daven*." Chani looked at me, her voice stronger now. "You should know, I have a whole program with Yossi. I bring him here three times a week, and I am teaching him to climb the monkey bars. It's taken weeks, but he is really progressing. My father says it's great for his coordination." Chani smiled at me. "Why don't you and Avramie join us? We can have a school! The Chani and Dena Playground School!" Chani pushed her glasses down to the tip of her nose and pulled her red hair into a knot at the top of her head. "Don't I look like a teacher?"

I couldn't help laughing at her.

PRIDE MEANS NOT HAVING TO HIDE

Well, that is how it all started. Ever since that day in the park, Chani and I have been best friends. We really did start that school, and Avramie and Yossi are really doing well. Avramie climbed to the top of the sliding board the other day!

My parents are really proud of me. Somehow, my father doesn't look so worried anymore. I guess that, besides being worried about Avramie, he was also worried about how it was affecting me. He must have thought that I wasn't making friends because of Avramie. But now, with Chani as my friend, I have more friends than I know what to do with. A lot of the girls come to the park now to help us with the Playground School, and I don't even mind.

The other day, Rachel Felder said to us, "You two are really lucky. Your brothers are so cute. All my little brother does is act bratty."

Chani and I just looked at each other and smiled. And in that smile was pain, understanding and . . . happiness.

One of the Gang

One of the Gang

"Rayfie, did you bring your *kugelach*?" Aryeh called from the back of the van.

Rayfie raised his hand with the five stones clutched tightly inside. "The name is Refael today!" he declared and grinned back at Aryeh.

Aryeh sighed. Rayfie looked so small and eager. Aryeh just hoped his first day in *yeshivah* would go well.

It was just two weeks before that Abba had called all the children into the living room and told them how Uncle Max and Aunt Riva, even though they weren't religious, had decided to send Rayfie to *yeshivah*. It seemed that ever since Rayfie had spent a *Shabbos* with Aryeh and his

STEPPING STONES

family, he'd been begging to be allowed to come live with his cousins and go to *yeshivah*. Finally, Uncle Max and Aunt Riva had agreed.

All the children had been very excited. Only Aryeh wasn't sure. "What grade will he be in, Abba?" Aryeh asked.

"We've decided to put him straight into the fifth grade," Abba replied. "He's had a tutor for the past few months."

"Abba, do you know what the fifth grade class is like? They'll laugh . . ." His voice trailed off as he caught Abba's warning glance. *Lashon hora* was not allowed.

"You're worried about whether they'll make him feel part of the group, Aryeh?" Abba asked.

Aryeh nodded.

"Well, I guess a lot of responsibility for that will lie on your shoulders, Aryeh. Having a seventh grader take him under his wing will surely be a good ice breaker."

And today, finally, was Rayfie's first day in *yeshivah*. Aryeh had taken Abba's words seriously. He'd taught Rayfie to play *kugelach* and reviewed *Chumash* with him. But the hardest part had been coaching Rayfie in baseball. Aryeh knew that baseball meant everything to the fifth grade class at *yeshivah*. If Rayfie could prove himself at baseball, then his funny accent and longish hair wouldn't matter. It was his only chance to become part of the group. And Aryeh loved baseball, too.

But Rayfie wasn't too excited about the idea. "I'm not really into baseball, Aryeh. In my old school we played

ONE OF THE GANG

handball a lot. We had a handball court, and I was one of the best at it."

Rayfie kicked at the bat lying next to him. "I mean, I'll continue practicing if you think that it's important . . ."

He'd let his sentence dangle, and Aryeh could just imagine him thinking, Is this what *yeshivah* is about?

It wasn't what *yeshivah* was all about, of course, but Aryeh was still sure Rayfie needed to learn baseball in order to fit in with the class.

His father's van swung into the school driveway and parked by the main entrance. "Good luck, Refael," Abba said as the children climbed out of the van.

"Good luck," the other children echoed.

Aryeh walked Rayfie to his classroom and introduced him to his new *rebbi*.

Rabbi Finkel gave Rayfie a friendly *shalom aleichem*, and as Aryeh left the room, he just managed to see Rabbi Finkel assigning Rayfie a seat next to David, one of the quieter boys in the fifth grade.

Aryeh's heart sank as he made his way back to his own seventh grade classroom.

Why hadn't Rabbi Finkel put him next to Moishy or Zevi, the two top athletes and leaders of the class? Aryeh wondered. He was sure David wouldn't be able to help Rayfie get "in" with the class.

The minute the recess bell rang, Aryeh jumped out of his seat and raced down to the fifth grade classroom.

Rayfie was standing near his desk, talking to David and Shimmy. They all looked up at Aryeh's entrance.

STEPPING STONES

David and Shimmy stepped back shyly, a little bit afraid of this big seventh grader. Rayfie looked startled.

"Come on, Rayf—uh, Refael. I'm going to play baseball with your class today."

"Okay, Aryeh, I'm coming."

The fifth graders were delighted to have a seventh grader play with them and promptly added Rayfie and Aryeh to a team. Aryeh tried as hard as he could to get Rayfie involved, but Rayfie just followed meekly behind him and struck out every time he was at bat.

The recess bell rang in the middle of the third inning. As the boys gathered up the bats and balls, Aryeh whispered into Rayfie's ear, "We'll practice some more tonight."

All during the afternoon, Aryeh worried about Rayfie. He knew that the fifth grade had another recess at three o'clock, but his own class didn't. Aryeh comforted himself with the thought that the fifth grade didn't usually play ball then. The break was too short. They'd probably just play *kugelach*, and Rayfie was okay at that.

On the way home in Abba's van, Rayfie was excited and happy.

"David and Shimmy want me to teach them how to play handball," he reported. "Shimmy said he'd help me with my *Chumash* at lunch. I want to bring my marbles tomorrow. David also has a collection." Rayfie's face shone. "Rabbi Finkel complimented me on my Hebrew handwriting, and I won the spelling contest!"

"Great, Rayfie," Aryeh was quick to compliment him.

ONE OF THE GANG

"But forget about studying at lunch with Shimmy. I'll help you with your *Chumash* tonight, and we really have to practice hitting the ball. I think Zevi and Moishy really like you, you just have to learn to bat a little better."

After supper, Aryeh dragged Rayfie out into the yard. Rayfie was reluctant even to try.

"Aryeh, I'm just not good at it," he insisted.

For a minute, Aryeh felt annoyed. Does this kid even realize what a sacrifice I'm making by giving up all my free time to help him? he thought to himself.

Aryeh was about to say something sharp to Rayfie when he remembered that he was supposed to be making him feel at home.

"Come on, Rayf—Refael, just a few balls."

The next day at recess, Shloimie, Aryeh's best friend, grabbed Aryeh's arm as he was about to run out of the room.

"Come on, Aryeh, how much time are you going to spend with the fifth grade? We need you for our team."

Aryeh shrugged him loose.

"Shloimie, I've got to help my cousin. I told you about him! He's new to the *yeshivah*, he doesn't know anyone, and we want him to like it. You know how it is."

"But, Aryeh," Shloimie insisted. "He has to make friends for himself. You can't do it for him. Give the fifth graders a chance to get to know him."

Aryeh didn't have time to argue. He had to be down in the yard by the time the fifth grade came out, so that he could get Rayfie on a team. Didn't Shloimie realize what

STEPPING STONES

an important job he was doing? Obviously, he had to make sure that Rayfie learned to play baseball, or he'd never be accepted by the guys in his class!

"Shloimie, you just don't understand," Aryeh repeated.

Aryeh cast a longing glance at his seventh grade class on the other side of the field. They were busily choosing up sides. Quickly, he turned to the fifth grade classroom. Rayfie was sitting on the floor shooting marbles with David and Shimmy. Another few boys were sitting around watching.

"Come on, Rayfie," Aryeh said, trying not to be annoyed. "Moishy and Zevi are already choosing up teams." He helped Rayfie gather up the marbles and stuff them in his desk. Then they ran out to the field.

In the third inning, Rayfie finally hit the ball.

"Terrific, Rayf, you're catching on," Aryeh said as he patted him on the shoulder. But somehow, Rayfie didn't look too excited.

"What was the best part of your day today, Refael?" Abba asked on the way home from school.

"I bet it was that hit you made," Aryeh guessed.

"That was fun," Rayfie mused. "But I think it was afternoon recess. I finished up a marble game with Shimmy and David. I really like those two boys, and we're thinking of opening up a club."

"That's great that you're making friends," Abba said with a smile.

"Yeah, I really like this *yeshivah*." Rayfie leaned back in his seat and started a find-an-out-of-state-license-plate

ONE OF THE GANG

game with Aryeh's brother Simchah.

Silly kid, doesn't even know what's good for him, Aryeh thought to himself. Tonight I'll really practice with him for a while. When he sees how good he can be, he'll like it and then he'll really get in with the guys in the class.

After dinner, Rayfie tried to avoid Aryeh's glance when he said, "Aryeh, I'm too tired to practice batting tonight. Let's do it tomorrow."

"Rayfie," Aryeh said impatiently, when suddenly he remembered that he was supposed to be making him feel comfortable. "All right, you get a good night's sleep. We'll try tomorrow." He smiled at Rayfie.

Abba was waiting for Aryeh when he came inside to get his book bag.

"You're really working hard with Rayfie, aren't you, Aryeh?" he asked.

"It's okay," Aryeh said. "It's worth it."

"You haven't been seeing too much of your own friends lately, have you?"

"Well, once he gets this baseball licked, I'll be able to let him manage on his own." Aryeh bent to take out his *Mishnayos*.

"Does he like the baseball, Aryeh?"

Aryeh was surprised at the question. "Well, right now he's not so good at it, but once he gets better, it will be worth it, because then he'll really get friendly with the top guys in his class."

"Aryeh," Abba's voice was soft. "I really appreciate all the effort you're putting into this. But whenever you help someone, you have to make sure that what you're doing is really for their own good."

Now what does that mean? Aryeh wondered as he opened his *Mishnayos*. Whose good would it be for if not Rayfie's? I certainly don't enjoy playing with a bunch of ten-year-olds, even if I do love baseball.

The next day at recess, before Aryeh had a chance to shoot out the door, Rabbi Horowitz called him over. He wanted to discuss the class's *tzeddakah* campaign, of which Aryeh was *gabbai*.

I don't have time for this, Aryeh thought impatiently. Rayfie needs me. But of course he couldn't say that to his *rebbe*.

Fifteen minutes later, with only two thirds of recess left, Aryeh was finally out on the field. He scanned the area but saw no sign of Rayfie among the baseball players. Suddenly, he heard some noise and laughter to his left.

"Hey, Rafi, is this the way you hit it?"

Rayfie was standing in the middle of a crowd of about six boys, demonstrating how to play handball against the red brick wall of the school building.

His face looked animated and excited. Aryeh thought back to how he'd looked playing baseball yesterday. And what was that they were calling him? Rafi—a real *yeshivah* nickname!

At that moment, Rayfie looked up and saw Aryeh. His face fell, and he turned around to hand the racquet to Shimmy.

All of a sudden, Aryeh felt tremendous relief. He

ONE OF THE GANG

flashed Rayfie a big smile, waved good-bye and then turned and ran off to the other end of the field. If he hurried, he could catch Shloimie and the rest of the gang before the last inning.

Strawberry Ice Cream

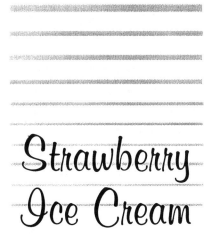

Strawberry Ice Cream

I UNCOILED THE TELEPHONE WIRE AND PULLED IT INTO the bedroom. I wanted to call my younger sister while I finished packing the suitcases.

"Hello, Simmy," I said into the receiver as I folded the last pile of clothes. "It's Yocheved. Listen, I'm giving you one last chance. Are you sure you still want us to come for *Pesach*? Are you sure you can handle my family's invasion?"

"Are you kidding?" Simmy squealed into my ear. "We are so excited that you are finally coming! The children don't stop talking about it. They can't wait to play with their cousins. Really, Yocheved, don't worry. I finished

STEPPING STONES

getting the kitchen ready for *Pesach* last night, and I'm going to start cooking tomorrow. I am really all organized."

"But Simmy," I protested, "right after *Pesach*, you are starting to teach at the seminary, and you told me that a magazine asked you to write an article for their next issue. When are you going to get a chance to prepare for all that if you have to cook for my whole family, besides yours?"

"Yocheved, don't worry!" Simmy's laugh rang clear through the telephone wires. "I'll have plenty of time to prepare, and anyway, cooking is no problem for me. I had an excellent teacher. Don't you remember the year you taught me to cook? It was the year that everything changed for me."

And suddenly I did remember. It was so many years ago. I was only fourteen then and Simmy only ten. I wonder if that really had been the turning point for this sister of mine, Simmy, who today was a happy mother of two, a very successful teacher and a writer as well.

In my mind's eye, I was once again fourteen years old and back in the big old kitchen at home. I had been helping my mother all day to get the kitchen ready for *Pesach*. We were almost finished putting all the *Pesach* dishes in order, when I asked Imma, "Are we going to start cooking tomorrow?"

I was really looking forward to our cooking session. Imma had promised me that this year she would let me do all the cooking for the *seder* myself. She would just be in the kitchen to supervise. We'd gone over all the recipes, and

STRAWBERRY ICE CREAM

I'd practiced them a few times. I could just imagine Aunt Leah's look of surprise when she heard that I had cooked the whole meal.

"Yes," Imma answered, "hopefully, tomorrow we'll start the cooking. I'm glad the school decided to start *Pesach* vacation early. I really need your help at home. I don't know how much work we'll get done with the little kids and Simmy home, though..." Imma let her sentence trail off.

Simmy! I thought to myself. What are we going to do about Simmy? I could feel the bubble of excitement inside me slowly melting away.

The funny thing is, I mused to myself as I started brushing my teeth and getting ready for bed, Simmy wasn't always such a problem. I remembered back about four years, before she started school. She was so different. She was always happy and excited about something, always bursting with some new idea or joke. She was a great organizer. When she was only six, she got all the little kids in the neighborhood together and made them an *Oneg Shabbos*. She was the first kid on the block to be riding a two-wheeler when everyone else was still hobbling along on training wheels.

Everyone used to laugh at all her *chachmos*, and Abba and Imma used to smile at each other whenever she came up with one of her deep, philosophical questions. I knew they were thinking, "Boy, this one is smart!" Who would believe that this was the same girl?

I glanced down at her before I got into my own bed.

STEPPING STONES

Even in her sleep she looked tense and uncomfortable. Her blanket was all rumpled, and she was curled up in a tight ball. She seemed even more unhappy since she heard that Uncle David and Aunt Leah were coming for *Pesach* with their children.

I sighed as I got into bed. The truth was, I knew exactly when the trouble had started. It was when Simmy was in the first grade. The problem was really very simple. Simmy could not read. It took a while for the teachers to catch on, because Simmy was so smart that she managed to keep everyone fooled. But now here she was, ten years old and in the fourth grade, and still unable to read well.

The doctors called it a fancy name. They said she had a learning disability. At school, Simmy was taken out for private classes, tutored, tested, and all the while, she just got angrier and sadder. She was used to being the organizer, the smart one, the one everyone admired, and now the kids called her "Dummy" behind her back.

I tossed and turned, trying to find a more comfortable position. Images of Simmy kept flitting through my mind, not letting me sleep. Simmy at the supper table, picking fights with everyone. Simmy standing alone in the school playground with a scowl on her face. Simmy throwing her reader on the floor and storming out. Simmy trying to learn how to cook and getting so frustrated with the written recipes that she ran crying to her room.

And now, our cousins were coming for the *seder*. I punched my pillow into a hard ball. Now I knew why Simmy was so upset about that. Of course, Dina would

STRAWBERRY ICE CREAM

also be there—smart, self-assured Dina, who was in Simmy's class at school. Simmy was probably picturing her sitting at the *seder* table, reading from the *Haggadah* in her loud, clear voice, answering all the questions and getting all the compliments. No wonder she didn't want them to come!

Suddenly, an idea hit me like a flash. I shot straight up in bed. What Simmy needed is to be good at something. She needed to be in charge like she used to be. Maybe I could convince Imma to let Simmy and me do all the cooking by ourselves, and then I would let Simmy take charge.

I jumped out of bed, grabbed my robe and recipe book and ran to the dining room table. The house was quiet, and the kitchen was dark. Abba and Imma had already gone up to bed.

I ran to my drawer for magic markers and a pack of big white paper. This time, I wouldn't frustrate Simmy with written recipes. I would draw her step by step pictures of each thing she had to do. She would be able to figure it all out herself.

I pulled out my orange magic marker and with a big flourish, began illustrating the carrot *kugel* recipe. It took me almost two hours to finish illustrating all the recipes. I was just looking over my handiwork, admiring the clear, bright pictures and thinking how happy they would make Simmy, when the clock struck two. Boy, was I tired!

I gathered up my magic markers and flew into bed. In ten minutes, I was fast asleep, dreaming of Simmy smiling

STEPPING STONES

and carrot *kugels* and matzah balls flying through the air.

The next morning, I cornered Imma bright and early, told her my plan and showed her the pictures I had drawn. Poor Imma! Her back ached, she was tired and nervous, but she just couldn't resist my enthusiasm.

"I guess I can leave it in your hands, Yocheved," she said. "Maybe it will really help Simmy."

Convincing Simmy was much more difficult. When I started telling her about us being in charge, I could see a glimmer of a smile on her face, but the minute I mentioned recipes, her face clouded over.

"No, I'm not helping you!" she yelled. "You can do it yourself or get that smart Dina to help you!"

"Simmy, just one minute," I coaxed. "Just look at the pictures I drew. You won't have to read a thing."

Simmy picked up the big white paper and looked at it suspiciously. "You mean, all I have to do is look at the pictures and do what it says?"

"That's all, Simmy, and you can do it all yourself. I'll just sit in the kitchen and supervise."

Simmy pointed to the first picture. "This means I peel ten carrots, right?"

"Boy, you figured that out fast, Simmy." I smiled at her. "Let's get started."

Simmy and I worked for six hours straight. Imma took the younger kids downstairs, read them stories and played with them, so we had the kitchen to ourselves. I'm sure Imma's thoughts were with us, but she kept her word and did not appear upstairs until we were all finished.

STRAWBERRY ICE CREAM

I really have to give my little sister credit. Talk about persistence! She just raced back and forth—from the carrot *kugel* to the *matzoh* balls, from the fish to the *pareve* ice cream. She didn't stop for a second! By the time the guests arrived, the kitchen was spotless and delicious aromas filled the house.

That afternoon, Aunt Leah couldn't believe that all the cooking was finished, but it wasn't until the *seder* that we revealed our secret.

Simmy was sitting next to me, and sure enough, Dina was in prime form. She read the *Haggadah* in a loud voice and asked lots of good questions. I could see Simmy sinking lower and lower into her seat. Her face was settling in the familiar, sullen expression.

Finally, Abba announced in a loud voice, "*Shulchan orech!*"

Simmy and I served the meal together. Everyone commented on how delicious everything was and how nice it looked. We just smiled. We brought out carp, neatly arranged on a platter with a bowl of homemade mayonnaise. Then came steaming chicken soup, golden brown chicken, carrot *kugel* and salads.

It wasn't until Simmy carried in the bowl of strawberry ice cream, decorated with cut-up strawberries, that I made my announcement.

"I want you all to know," I said, "that the meal you were just served was cooked and baked entirely by Simmy Katz. She made everything herself."

Aunt Leah's mouth dropped open. Even Abba looked

STEPPING STONES

surprised. "Come on, Yocheved, you must have helped her. She couldn't have done this all by herself!"

"No," I said, shaking my head. "I just sat there and watched. Simmy did the whole thing!"

"Amazing!" Aunt Leah said, shaking her head admiringly. "A ten-year-old girl who can cook a whole meal for twelve people! Simmy, you are remarkable!"

"I don't think I've ever peeled a carrot in my whole life," Dina added, smiling at Simmy. "How did you do it?"

I looked at Simmy standing there, with her big bowl of pink ice cream, her face glowing with pride, and I thought, Who knows what doors are open to her now that she is free to let the real Simmy shine through?

Simmy's voice on the other end of the line brought me out of my reverie. "You didn't just teach me how to cook, though, Yocheved. You showed me that if I tried hard enough, with Hashem's help, I could do almost anything. That was when I really began to try."

I was still lost in my thoughts. It was hard to believe it was almost fifteen years later. Here I was, packing my suitcase to go and visit my sister for *Pesach* with my own family.

"Yocheved," I could hear the smile in Simmy's voice. "Should we have strawberry ice cream for dessert at the *seder*? Do your children like it as much as we used to?"

Growing Pains

Growing Pains

THERE WAS A SHADOW IN THE KITCHEN OF THE Archman house. It lingered over the walls and around the furniture. Even when the sun shone, Orlee could still see it, hovering darkly over the room, hanging almost in a cloud over her mother's rocking chair.

Once, Orlee had loved that rocking chair. It had been the place where her mother cuddled and rocked her when she skinned her knee, lost her ball or just hadn't had a good day. When Orlee, Neelie and Aaron would all come barging in from school, tired and hungry, their mother would always be sitting there, doing her mending and smiling her greeting. And the kids would sit at the table, eating their after-school snacks and vying with each other to be the first to tell their mother about their day.

But since the shadow had descended on the house, Orlee hated the rocking chair. Her mother had been sitting there the day the phone had rung with the news that her brother Aaron had been in an accident. When the *levayah* and *shivah* were finally over, her mother had moved the chair into the corner of the kitchen, away from the sun pouring in through the picture window.

When her mother sat and rocked now, her face was white and pinched, her eyes dark and big. When they all came trooping in after school, tired and hungry, their snack still waited on the table and their mother still smiled in greeting. But to Orlee, it seemed like a shadow had crept into her mother's eyes and smile. And when Orlee heard the chair creaking late into the night, she knew that her mother was still sitting there in the dark kitchen, staring blankly out the big picture window. Orlee needed to cover her head with the pillow to shut out the sound.

She would lie in bed, stiff and straight, and try to sleep while images of Aaron slipped through her mind. Aaron, tall and strong, with laughing brown eyes and crooked dimples. Aaron, who could keep them all in stitches as he told them about the ordinary things that happened to him that day. Aaron, who had teased her and Neelie mercilessly but was always there when they needed him.

It was Aaron who had taught her to ice skate, forcing her out on the rink over and over again, even though she was afraid of falling. And in the end, when she had made

GROWING PAINS

her first tremulous journey alone around the rink, feeling free as a bird, it was Aaron who was waiting to congratulate her and tease her about how frightened she had looked.

On the way home that day, Aaron had said, "You see, Orlee, sometimes the things that are hardest to do give us the most pleasure in the end. It is called growing pains." And he was right, because ice skating soon became her favorite sport. Even now, when it was hard to fall asleep, she would imagine herself whizzing around the rink, the wind in her hair, bending and swaying around the other skaters, and the image would make sleep come faster.

But ice skating was only a memory now. Orlee hadn't been to the rink since before Aaron had died, and she knew she would never go back. She knew she couldn't even broach the topic with Imma.

Since the accident, her mother didn't let the children out of her sight, except to go to school. Even when they played out in the yard, Imma sat by the window, watching them and waiting for them to come in again. The younger children, Eli, Shani and Moishy, were too small to go anywhere by themselves anyway, and Orlee understood her mother too well to argue. But Orlee knew that Neelie was chafing at the bit.

Orlee still remembered the day when Neelie had talked her mother into letting her go on a class trip to an amusement park. Orlee had watched the proceedings half admiringly and half disdainfully. Neelie had waited until Imma was alone in the kitchen. Then, her freckles dancing

STEPPING STONES

and her short straight hair flying, Neelie had begun her pitch. She had begged and pleaded and argued and discussed, until her mother, with a tired half smile, had agreed.

Neelie had skipped out of the kitchen joyously, and Orlee had been jealous. She knew she could never have done what Neelie had done. Neelie was like Aaron used to be, peppy and full of life. Nothing could get her down. Although she lived in the same house as Orlee, it seemed that Neelie lived inside a bubble of light where the shadow couldn't touch her.

But when the day of the trip finally came, Orlee was glad it wasn't she who had caused her mother that pain. Neelie had said she would be home at four o'clock. By three-thirty, her mother was sitting in her rocking chair, her *Tehillim* in her lap, her eyes growing darker and the tempo of her chair going faster and faster. Finally, Neelie burst through the door at four-thirty, breathless, apologetic and full of stories about how the bus had broken down.

Imma hadn't scolded, but that night, Orlee had heard the creak of the rocking chair until late into the night, and she had strengthened her resolve to spare her mother.

And that was the role Orlee played now. She came straight home from school every day and helped her mother with the children, making sure to keep them in the yard and trying not to let Moishy do anything more dangerous than climb the tree. Orlee had banished the thought of ice-skating from her mind, and when her

GROWING PAINS

friends talked about getting together after school, she would turn her head away, dig in her heels, and think of the dark circles under Imma's eyes. Then she didn't even want to go anymore.

Sometimes she wondered what Aaron would think if he could see her and Imma now. She knew he wouldn't like it. He probably would hate it, but then again, he wouldn't even be aware of the secret pact she had with her mother, the pact that had never been verbalized. It was almost as if they felt that by keeping the family within the tight circle of the house, within the usual sphere of activities of school, house, homework, dinner and bed, they were protecting them from any further harm.

Orlee was sure that the shadow would govern their lives forever—until the day of the fire changed everything.

The day of the fire was also the day of a neighbor's *barmitzvah*. Orlee's parents were invited, but of course, her mother refused to go. Orlee's father tried convincing Imma that it would be good to get out. He said that Orlee and Neelie were perfectly capable of babysitting and that they would only be gone a few hours anyway. But Imma could not be convinced. Even Orlee tried a few tentative persuasions, but when she saw how adamant her mother was, she gave up. In the end, Abba finally left by himself. Imma took up her position by the window, watching Shani in the sandbox, and Orlee went upstairs to supervise Eli and Moishy who were playing in the next room.

Orlee sat in the big lounge chair by the window, a book in her lap, enjoying the cool breeze wafting through the

STEPPING STONES

screen. In the background, she could vaguely hear the sound of her brothers deeply involved in a game of checkers. She was glad they were keeping busy and giving her a chance to read. It was good to be able to relax like this and lose herself in a book.

Suddenly, Eli's voice shocked her out of her reverie. He stood at the door to her room shaking like a leaf but still talking quietly so that Imma wouldn't hear. "Orlee, Moishy was playing with matches! There is a big fire! Come quick!"

For a moment, as Orlee sat there almost rooted in place, Moishy's freckled, eager face merged with Aaron's in her mind. Then she was running, knocking over the lounge chair, dropping her book and spinning through the door.

Orlee stood at the top of the stairs staring at the door of Moishy's room, mesmerized at the growing wall of orange and blue flames licking at the sides of the walls. She heard Moishy whimper, and she could see his little face peering at her over the wall of flames, a book of matches in his hand and a defiant look on his face. He still didn't realize he was trapped.

Orlee sized up the situation in an instant. "Stay there, Moishy," she called. Forcing her voice to stay calm, she grabbed Eli by the shoulders and propelled him towards the stairs. "Go downstairs and tell Imma what happened, and then go outside and wait on the lawn for me. I'll bring Moishy down in a minute."

When Orlee was sure Eli was on the way, she ran back down the hall and grabbed a blanket from Eli's bed in the

GROWING PAINS

next room. "Hurry, hurry," she urged herself as she dragged the blanket back into Moishy's room. She felt like she was trying to move under water. Her legs just wouldn't move quickly enough, and as she ran, Aaron's face floated before her eyes.

The flames were higher now, and she could just see the tip of Moishy's *yarmulka* over the wall of flames. His cries were getting louder.

"Moishy," she called. "I'm coming, don't move."

She felt the flames grow hotter as she neared them, rising up and singeing her chin. With all the energy she possessed, she beat heavily with her blanket, while willing the flames to part. Her mother's face swam before her eyes as she beat on the flames with strength she never knew she had.

Suddenly, she was on the other side, and Moishy was in her arms at the window. She could see Eli and Shani on the lawn surrounded by neighbors, and Neelie, who must have come back early from her friend's house. Neelie was standing under the window, her eyes big and her freckles dark against her white face, her arms outstretched as if she would catch Orlee.

"Jump, Orlee!" she called. "Jump!"

Orlee pulled Moishy up on the window sill, but still she hesitated. She heard the ringing of the fire engines as if through a fog. She wasn't afraid to jump. It wasn't even that high. Aaron had climbed out of this window a number of times when he couldn't be bothered to use the front door. Still she hesitated. Where was Imma? Then she saw

95

STEPPING STONES

her across the street. She could see Imma straining towards the house, towards her and Moishy, with two neighbors holding her back, trying to restrain her. Orlee was sure that the scene in front of her eyes would be etched in her mind forever. And then, as the fire engines swooped into her street, Orlee jumped, with Moishy clutched tightly in her arms.

Later when the firemen had finally left, the rooms had been straightened up, the neighbors had finished milling around and being helpful, and the children had dropped off to sleep, Orlee crept into her own dark bedroom on the ground floor. The room still reeked slightly of smoke. Orlee got into bed and under the covers. She lay stiff and still and stared up at the ceiling.

Orlee realized that the pact hadn't worked. For the past few months, she had given every ounce of her being to keeping her side of the bargain. No matter how hard it had been, she had struggled to keep the children within the tight circle—and it hadn't worked. Through the dark, her ears picked up a sound. She pulled her blanket over her head, but the sound reached her anyway. It was the rocking chair.

Slowly at first, then with increasing strength, the first tears since Aaron's death began seeping between Orlee's eyelids. She stuffed her blanket into her mouth and bit down on it, but she couldn't stop the sobs rising in her throat.

There was a rustle from the other side of the room. Orlee bit harder on the blanket, willing herself to stop. She

GROWING PAINS

heard Neelie's feet pattering across the carpet, and she buried her head deeper into the pillow. Neelie would never understand why she was crying, now that the danger was over, and neither did she herself understand it. But the tears wouldn't stop. She felt Neelie's hand on her shoulder. She braced herself for Neelie's rebuke, but Neelie didn't say anything. Neelie just stroked her sister's shoulder gently and then she whispered softly in Orlee's ear, "Cry, Orlee, cry. It will be good for you."

Good for me? Orlee thought even as her sobs grew louder. How can crying be good for me? But then she couldn't think anymore; she just let her tears pour out.

After she couldn't cry any longer, Orlee just lay there spent, with Neelie's arm around her, feeling strangely relaxed and calm. She was just thinking of getting up to wash her face, when the door clicked open quietly and someone flicked on the light.

"I thought I would find the two of you in here," Imma's voice said. She sounded so normal and natural that both Orlee and Neelie turned in surprise.

Imma pulled a chair out from under the desk. She pulled the chair close to Orlee's bed and reached for her hand. With her other hand, she patted Neelie's knee.

Orlee looked searchingly at her mother's face. Something was different. Imma looked somehow calmer and more herself, like before Aaron had died. But Orlee couldn't quite place the difference.

"We learned an important lesson tonight, Orlee, didn't we?" Orlee's mother said. "We learned that no matter how

STEPPING STONES

hard we try, we can't protect the people we love. It is all in Hashem's hands." She paused and looked lovingly at Neelie. "It is something Abba and Neelie have been trying to teach us for a long time. It is what Aaron would have wanted us to learn. We have to lead normal lives, Orlee. I can't keep you children near me all the time. I have to let you go. I must remember that Hashem loves you even more than I do and that He will take care of you better than I ever could."

Orlee opened her mouth to speak, but she did not know what to say.

"Orlee," Imma said with a smile, her voice growing soft, "I heard that your class goes ice-skating together every Sunday. I want you to go, too." She squeezed Orlee's hand tightly. "It won't be easy for us, you know." Her voice broke and then she strengthened it again. She smiled a shaky smile. "All we have to do is try. Aaron would have called it growing pains."

And Orlee, squeezing her mother's hand back, finally recognized the difference in her mother's face. Maybe it wasn't the same light, but a brightness of some sort was pushing away the shadow in her eyes.

Training a Porcupine

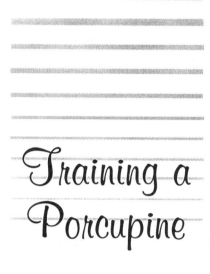

Training a Porcupine

*Y*ITZI COULD COUNT AT LEAST FIVE AWFUL THINGS that had happened since they moved to Park City. They had all been delighted at the idea of moving out of the little town they had lived in since Yitzi was born to a big city where Yitzi and Yael would be able to go to a decent *yeshivah*. Dad would have his pick of *minyanim* and *shiurim*, and Mom would have friends on her own wavelength. When Dad had gotten that transfer, it had seemed like a dream come true.

Yitzi looked around the kitchen and snorted to himself. Some dream, he thought. This is more like a nightmare! Yitzi was sure that things couldn't get much worse. It

STEPPING STONES

wasn't just that things in school were going downhill, but even at home things didn't look too good.

Yitzi's father was bent over his breakfast plate, perusing the account books that lay before him on the table and always keeping one eye on the clock. Yitzi's mother, her face wan and pale, sat opposite him, sipping her coffee slowly, her eyes far away. Yitzi could tell by the stack of empty boxes standing in the corner that she had been up all night finishing the unpacking.

Yitzi got up to get some more milk and scraped his chair against the floor. His father glanced up from his books for a minute and gave him an annoyed look before returning to his work.

Things used to be so different, Yitzi thought as he opened the refrigerator door. He thought back to what breakfast used to be like back in Tellton. It was like a different family altogether. His mother would be humming happily under her breath as she prepared their lunch bags. His father would be relaxed and cheerful, teasing Yael about her constant chatter, exchanging news with his mother and discussing Yitzi's schedule with him. In those days, his father was never in a rush. It seemed he always had time for a joke, a talk and an extra cup of coffee.

Yitzi brought the milk back to the table, being careful not to scrape the chair again. The contrast couldn't be more stark. Since they had arrived in their new home, it seemed like his father had turned into a shadow. He left early in the mornings, came back late at night, worked on Sundays and spent his time at home bent over office work. He

TRAINING A PORCUPINE

insisted that it was temporary and that it took time to get into a new job, but to the rest of the family, it was like a stranger had moved in with them. A tense, irritable, aloof stranger who demanded lots of quiet and no disturbances.

It wasn't that Yitzi minded being quiet. He wasn't a great talker anyway. But he desperately needed to discuss his school situation with his father, or rather with the father he used to have. By the time his father felt settled in the new job and came out of his working trance, it might be too late.

In fact, just thinking about school made Yitzi's stomach tighten. He scanned the kitchen for something else to think about and his glance rested on Yael. He smiled in spite of himself. It seemed like nothing could squelch Yael's enthusiasm, not the new school, not their father's being so busy, nor anything else. In between noisy slurps of her cereal, she was busily recounting some incident from school, totally unaware that no one was really listening. Her brown eyes, so like his own, sparkled and snapped, and her brown, curly pony tail bounced along behind her, emphasizing each point.

Just then, something Yael was saying made him tune into the conversation. He was just in time to hear the tail end of her sentence.

"So they are planning the *Chol Hamoed* trip already," Yael said, and suddenly, excitement charged through Yitzi like an electric bolt.

Sukkos! Sukkos was coming. Things would have to change over *Sukkos*. Back at home, *Sukkos* had always been

STEPPING STONES

their most special holiday, with their big *sukkah* out in the backyard, the constant stream of guests and Mom's scrumptious delicacies. It had also been Dad's favorite holiday. He had always spent the whole week out in the *sukkah*, hating to come in, even when it rained. Things will have to change over *Sukkos*, Yitzi thought. Dad will have to relax, and maybe he will be able to help me with my school problems. And best of all, there will be no school at all for that whole week!

"Hey, Dad, when are we going to start building the *sukkah* this year?" Yitzi asked, cutting right into the middle of Yael's sentence and ignoring her outburst of indignation.

Mr. Kurtner pushed his chair back and stuffed his papers into the briefcase that stood waiting on the chair next to him.

"You think that I have time to build a *sukkah* this year?" he replied. "We will use the *shul's sukkah*." His face softened when he noticed Yitzi's shocked expression. "Why do you think we moved to the city and bought a home so close to the *shul*? I will be working all through *Chol Hamoed* anyway."

Yael, uninhibited as usual, let out a wail. "But, Daddy, you can't mean that! I need a *sukkah*! All my friends are going *sukkah* hopping, and I won't be able to invite them to come see ours!"

Yael's father smiled a tired smile, his hand on the doorknob. "I'm sorry, pumpkin, but that is just the way it will have to be, at least until I get myself settled in this new

TRAINING A PORCUPINE

job. It isn't so easy, picking up a family, buying a house in a new neighborhood and starting a new job. We will just have to do without a *sukkah* this year." And with a wave of his hand, he was gone.

No *sukkah* for the Kurtner family? Yitzi couldn't believe it. Things were going from bad to worse. He pushed back his chair, glanced at his mother, and excused himself. He had to get out to the back yard to think a little before he left for school.

Yitzi heard the screen door click, and he felt the ground vibrate with Yael's footsteps. She knew just where to find him. In the barely two weeks that they had been there, he had already found himself a special spot behind the bushes in the back yard, under the shade of a tall oak tree.

Yael flung herself on the ground beside him, her face all puckered up. Yitzi knew that she would be crying in a minute, and sure enough, as she started talking, her sobs came pouring out, shaking her whole body. Yitzi could barely make out her words as they came tumbling out between gasping sobs, punctuated by thumps on the ground with her pudgy fists. ". . . Everything is different . . . Daddy has no time . . . Mommy is tired . . . Even you aren't the same . . . You're always in a bad mood . . . and now, not even a *sukkah* . . ."

Yael's sobs threatened to reach a crescendo, and Yitzi reached over and patted her shoulder clumsily. "Ssshh, Yael, crying won't change anything. As soon as Daddy gets settled in his job, everything will be back to normal," he said, sounding unconvincing even to his own ears.

105

STEPPING STONES

"Yeah, but who knows when that will be?" Yael wailed, her tears starting anew. "Can you imagine what *Sukkos* will be like? You and Daddy rushing to the *shul's sukkah* to eat your meals while Mommy and I eat at home? Daddy sleeping the whole day to rest up for his job . . . Mommy won't even enjoy cooking all her *Yom Tov* specialties when we can't eat together with lots of guests . . ."

"It won't be like that at all," Yitzi answered weakly. "And besides, it takes time to become part of a new community. Whom are we supposed to invite anyway?"

"Well, even if we did have someone," Yael countered, "you can't invite them without a *sukkah*. And you are just sitting there, accepting it all calmly." Yael turned red, teary eyes on him accusingly. "You didn't even try and change Daddy's mind."

"Can't you see?" Yitzi began, wondering how to explain things to Yael.

"See what?" Yael asked angrily. "All I see is that this family is falling apart and you're not doing anything about it!"

Now it was Yitzi's turn to glare. "What do you mean? What am I supposed to do about it?"

"Why don't you . . . Why don't you . . . Why don't you build a *sukkah* yourself?" Yael finished triumphantly. "That would be doing something instead of just sitting there." Her brown eyes began to sparkle again through her tears. "You could use all those old boards lying back there in Mr. Davis's yard, and you could get *s'chach* from someone who is trimming his tree. I bet Daddy would love

TRAINING A PORCUPINE

it! Maybe we could even find some guests to invite . . ." Yael's voice trailed off in dreamy speculation.

For a moment, even Yitzi caught her excitement. It would be great to have their own *sukkah*. And he was sure that if they had a *sukkah* his father would enjoy it, too. He could just imagine his father's surprise and his mother's pleasure. And it would be fun trying to build it by himself!

"You would have to ask Mr. Davis if you could use the wood back there and if you could use the fence as one wall," Yael said suddenly. "Do you think he would let you?"

Yitzi's excitement started to flicker. "Forget it," he told himself. "Old Mr. Davis won't even give us the time of day, let alone the use of the boards." He thought for a moment. It seemed like such a pity to give up on such a great idea just because of grouchy Mr. Davis.

"And I think Sarah told me that Mr. Marcus gives out free *s'chach* to the community from his tree prunings," Yael continued, unaware of Yitzi's hesitations. "Isn't Yoni Marcus in your class? You can ask him today."

Yitzi's stomach did a flip flop. Yoni Marcus! The thought of asking Yoni Marcus for anything made his face burn. Yitzi jumped up from the ground. If Yael only knew! Yoni Marcus thought Yitzi was the biggest nerd that ever lived. Yitzi wouldn't ask him for anything. He reached down and grabbed his book bag.

"Forget it, Yael. It was a great idea, but it just won't work." And then to get that sad puppy look off her face, he said, "Come on, I'll race you to the corner."

STEPPING STONES

All through the morning in school, Yitzi's thoughts kept returning to Yael's idea. The truth was, it was a great notion. He was sure things really would change if he could manage to carry it out. It seemed ridiculous that his fear of old Mr. Davis, and especially his fear of Yoni, should get in his way.

But by the time the end of the day rolled around, Yitzi was convinced, one hundred percent, that he could never ask Yoni for anything.

It was after lunch and the boys were all waiting around in the classroom for Mr. Cler to come in. Yitzi was sitting at his desk, pretending to be engrossed in checking his math homework and hoping that the class clowns would forget about him for the day. In all the stories he'd read, the hero would laugh along with the people who were making fun of him, and they would all end up being best of friends. But somehow, Yitzi just couldn't do it. No matter how determined he was to loosen up and be friendly, whenever one of those cool, confident, big city *yeshivah* boys approached him, he would just feel himself stiffen. For the life of him, he couldn't think of one normal thing to say.

If that alone had been the problem, he could have handled it. The guys would have just assumed that he was shy or quiet, and they would have left him alone until he adjusted. The real problem was that while Yitzi couldn't think of anything good to say, he always did manage to say the wrong thing. Somehow, whenever one of the boys came over and actually said something that sounded

TRAINING A PORCUPINE

halfway civil, he never thought they were really sincere and, in spite of himself, always managed to say something nasty in return. Afterwards, he could kick himself around the block about it, but there was nothing he could do. What was said was said. By now, he seemed to be the butt of every joke.

Out of the corner of his eye, Yitzi noticed Shimon sitting down next to him. "Oh, no," he groaned to himself. He already had Shimon pegged as the class *tzaddik*, and all he needed right now was to be the target of another *mitzvah* missile. He could feel himself tensing up.

"Hey, Yitzi, how about coming over to my house this afternoon to study for that *Chumash* test?" Shimon asked in a voice which, to Yitzi, just oozed fake friendliness.

Yitzi hesitated a minute before answering. He knew it wasn't Shimon's fault that he felt left out and lonely, that all his dreams of being part of the crowd in this new school were slowly being shattered. Yet Shimon's overly sweet voice and his condescending manner turned Yitzi's stomach. After all, Yitzi reasoned to himself, why else would Shimon want me, the most backward boy in the class, to study with him, if not because I was his latest *mitzvah* case?

Almost against his will, he heard himself answering, or rather growling, "Thanks, Shimon, but pick someone else as your next *mitzvah* case."

The minute he said it, he was sorry. Yitzi noticed the flush of red slowly creeping up Shimon's cheeks, and he said to himself, Well, Yitzi, this time you really blew it. This was probably the last emissary. Now you can really

STEPPING STONES

resign yourself to the role of class outcast.

But the class wasn't finished with him yet. Yitzi realized, only too late, that quite a few boys had apparently been listening to the little exchange between him and Shimon. David, who was sitting on the floor in front of the room, playing *kugelach* with Yoni Marcus, called out, "Forget it, Shimon, don't bother wasting your time with him. He is like a porcupine. I have no idea why he thinks he is better than the rest of us, but just try to be nice to him and you get a quill shot at you."

Yoni looked up from where he was trying to do "fivesies" and said, "Maybe he's like a *sabra*, David. You know, prickly on the outside and soft on the inside."

David laughed, "Maybe he's like a toothpick. Prickly at both ends, but useful at times—like for a few laughs."

Yoni was warming up to the game. "Or maybe he's like a . . ."

But just then the bell rang, and Mr. Cler strode in. Yitzi was spared from further speculation on his prickly nature.

Yitzi forced himself to concentrate on what the teacher was saying. Just because you're the class outcast doesn't mean you have to be the class dunce also, he told himself fiercely, staring at the page in his math book with eyes that he refused to allow to tear.

Somehow, he made it through the day, keeping a straight blank face, determined not to let anyone know he was squirming inside. When the last bell finally rang, he shot out of his chair like a stone from a slingshot. Not until he was safely ensconced under the oak tree at home, with

TRAINING A PORCUPINE

a handful of the chocolate chip cookies his mother had left for him on the kitchen table, did he let himself relax.

Porcupine. *Sabra*. Toothpick. The words kept hammering away in his brain, as the picture of that day's scene kept replaying itself in his head. Yitzi had to admit that they were right in a way. He had been acting pretty prickly and grouchy. But he couldn't believe how off the mark David was. It certainly wasn't because he thought he was better than everybody else. They should have called me armadillo, Yitzi thought to himself suddenly. The thorns are just my armor—and I wish I knew how to retract them!

Yitzi rose and paced up and down under the oak tree. Actually, he remembered reading a book about a boy who had found a baby porcupine and brought it up, training it as it grew. According to the book, the porcupine had turned into a sweet, gentle pet who never hurt his owner with its quills. He chuckled to himself, I guess I'm just an untrainable porcupine.

Yitzi kicked a stone away from his path. He was sick of thinking about it any more. That's it, kid, he said to himself. Just resign yourself to being an outcast. Think about something else now.

Involuntarily, Yael's idea popped back into his head. If he could get involved in building the *sukkah*, that would be great. It would give him something else to think about besides school. Besides, it would be a lot of fun, and maybe his father really would relax and have more time for him.

Yitzi glanced around the yard with a well-practiced frown. Now, where would I build the *sukkah* if I decide to

111

STEPPING STONES

do it? he wondered. His eyes fell on the pile of boards on Mr. Davis's side of the fence and he groaned. He'd forgotten all about Mr. Davis. How cou'ld he ever convince Mr. Davis to let them use those boards and to use their joint fence as one wall? Mr. Davis was impossible. Yitzi couldn't imagine him ever agreeing to anything.

Now that is a real porcupine for you, he thought. He smiled as he remembered the first time they had met Mr. Davis. He, his mother and Yael had been exploring the back yard during the first week they had moved in, when suddenly, seemingly out of nowhere, a noise from the other side of the fence had made them all turn in surprise.

Mr. Davis was leaning over the fence, shaking his fist at them, looking for all the world like a grizzly bear. His white hair stood up in tufts over most of his head with some bare spots in between, like a toothbrush with some bristles missing. His moustache, short and trimmed though it was, stood out sharply, and his glasses had slipped down to the end of his nose. He brandished his pipe at them with one hand while clenching the edge of the fence with his other white-knuckled fist.

"I knew it!" he half croaked, half yelled. "I knew having a family with a bunch of kids next door would make my ulcer worse." He clutched his stomach. "You just be careful," he continued, still brandishing his pipe, "if you make any noise while I am sleeping, I'll, I'll . . ." He pounded his fist on the edge of the fence while thinking of a satisfying conclusion to his threat.

Mrs. Kurtner had rallied herself by that time. She

TRAINING A PORCUPINE

stepped forward and said softly, with the smile that people always said could charm birds out of trees, "Why, how nice to meet you, Mr. Davis. You must be our new neighbor. Please do tell me which are your rest hours, and I'll be sure to keep the children out of the yard during that time."

Mr. Davis sputtered for a minute, like a boiling kettle that had had the flame turned off underneath it, and said, "It's nice to meet you too, ma'am. It's just these kids that I'm worried about . . ." He looked strangely defenseless once he'd stopped yelling, and Yitzi almost felt bad for him. He was so struck by how tame Mr. Davis had become that he had resolved to be extra careful not to disturb him.

Yitzi and Yael soon discovered, though, that Mr. Davis's friendly demeanor only made an appearance when one of their parents was around. Whenever Yitzi and Yael met him by themselves, Mr. Davis always glowered at them from under bushy eyebrows, and no amount of winning smiles from Yitzi or cheerful hellos from Yael seemed to help.

Now, lying back under his tree, Yitzi marvelled at how similar he was to Mr. Davis. He could imagine that the boys in his class were just as perplexed by his behavior as he was by Mr. Davis's. Also, they probably couldn't understand why, no matter what they said to him, Yitzi just snapped back.

The difference was, Yitzi realized, that while he was sure he had nothing to offer those boys, he knew he really needed Mr. Davis. He needed the use of his fence boards,

113

STEPPING STONES

and more importantly, he needed Mr. Davis to tell him how he used to build his *sukkah*, so that he could use the same plan. There was no doubt about it! If he really wanted to build a *sukkah*, he was going to have to learn to train porcupines himself.

Ten minutes later, Yitzi was marching resolutely up the path to Mr. Davis's house, fully equipped with a jug of mint tea—the kind his mother always used to make for Uncle Bernie when his ulcer was acting up—and a plate of freshly baked cinnamon cookies. Without stopping to let the butterflies in his stomach convince him to turn around, Yitzi rapped smartly on Mr. Davis's front door.

The door opened so quickly that Yitzi was sure Mr. Davis had been watching his approach through the window.

"What do you want?" he rasped out before Yitzi had a chance to open his mouth.

Yitzi hesitated for a second, wondering how to begin. He was sure Mr. Davis didn't want to be considered a *mitzvah* case, either, a "be-nice-to-the-grouchy-old-neighbor" project, but he was counting on the gifts he had brought to soften him up a little.

Suddenly, he had a brainstorm. Mr. Davis wanted to feel needed too. Yitzi was sure of it! He took a step forward, lifted his chin and looked straight at his neighbor.

"Mr. Davis," he said firmly, "I need your advice." Before Mr. Davis had a chance to reply, he placed the cookies and tea on the little table standing near the front door. "My mother sent this over to you. She said mint tea

TRAINING A PORCUPINE

is particularly soothing to ulcers. But the real reason I came was that I need your help. Can I come in and talk to you?" Yitzi's glance never wavered.

Mr. Davis looked from the fragrant mint tea and cookies to the boy in front of him, who seemed totally unfazed by his fierce glare.

"Well, young man," he said. "You can thank your mother for me. As for helping you, I'm sure I don't know what you would need from me, but whatever it is, you'd better tell me right here. There is no need to come in."

Boy, Yitzi thought, this will be harder than I thought. Am I as prickly as Mr. Davis? Well, no one ever said porcupine training was easy.

Yitzi took a deep breath. He would tell him the story straight, and if that didn't help, he would consider himself defeated. He started at the beginning, explaining why they had moved to the city, about his Dad's strenuous new job, about the kind of *sukkah* they use to have at home. He told him about how upset Yael had been that she couldn't invite her friends over and how sure he was that if they had a *sukkah* it would make his father more relaxed and get the family back together. And—here came the clincher—he told him about the idea of using the old boards out in the back.

"I don't know," Mr. Davis said, when Yitzi had finally finished. He beetled his brows again. "Those boards out there are excellent lumber. I used to build my own *sukkah* out there. It's only now with my arthritis and stomach pains," he gestured towards the mint tea, "that I use the

STEPPING STONES

shul's sukkah myself. I'm not sure that I want some young pipsqueak tinkering around with my boards."

Yitzi racked his brains. He could tell that Mr. Davis was wavering. What could he do to swing the balance in his favor? What was really bothering Mr. Davis? He guessed it was seeing his *sukkah* being taken over. Maybe that was it, Yitzi thought.

"You know what, Mr. Davis," Yitzi burst out, "I have a great idea. Why don't we be partners? You supply the lumber and tell me how to do it, and I'll do the building. Then we will both use the *sukkah*."

Mr. Davis's face lit up like someone had turned the light on behind those grizzly eyebrows. He harumphed loudly. "Well, young man, why don't you sit down and have some cookies with me while we discuss the building plans?"

Yitzi allowed himself a small smile as he sat down. He was a successful porcupine trainer after all. But as he reached for a cookie, he reminded himself that the more difficult porcupine training was still to come. He knew he still had to retrain himself.

Two days later, Yitzi stood in the back yard and looked around. He was exhilarated. Despite having worked for four solid hours, lugging boards, sawing beams and hammering nails under Mr. Davis's strict attention, he could still feel the energy coursing through his veins.

The *sukkah* looked beautiful. He never would have believed it would turn out so well. The walls were straight and sturdy, and the *sukkah* itself looked like a compact

TRAINING A PORCUPINE

square box. All it needed was some nice green pine needles to make it look like a real picture book *sukkah*. He wondered what his father would say.

He looked across the yard at Mr. Davis. Mr. Davis was comfortably planted in their green lawn chair, a glass of mint tea in his hand, directing operations with a satisfied look on his face. Yitzi grinned to himself. The prickly porcupine seemed to have disappeared, and in its stead was a kind, gracious grandfather type who only showed occasional glimpses of his old sourness.

Yael was crouched in the corner, busily tightening some screws. She had sawdust in her pony tail, making her look prematurely gray. There were smudges on her cheek and she'd banged her thumb with a hammer three times, but she was still going strong.

"You're okay, Yael," he said to her. "Don't forget this was all your idea."

Yael ducked her head. She was trying to look modest, but her delighted expression gave her away.

"When are you going to get the *s'chach* from Mr. Marcus?" she asked suddenly.

In an instant, all Yitzi's exhilaration slithered out of him like air hissing out of a balloon. This morning, when he had started to build the *sukkah*, he had resolutely put all thoughts of Yoni Marcus and the *s'chach* out of his mind. After hours of twisting and turning the night before, he had come to the conclusion that if even grouchy old Mr. Davis had been trained, there was hope for anyone—even himself.

STEPPING STONES

The trick was, he had decided, to remember that everyone has something to offer. All you have to do is retract your quills and give the other person a chance to get to know you. The question was, could he still convince Yoni Marcus that he was worth getting to know?

Well, there was only one way to find out. No use putting it off any longer, he told himself. It's either now or never.

"Right now, Yael," he said, forcing himself to sound calm and cheerful. "You want to come?"

Yael jumped eagerly to her feet. Yitzi called to Mr. Davis to tell him where they were going, and they were on their way.

We're heading straight for the lion's den, Yitzi thought grimly. Maybe, since it is such a nice, sunny day, Yoni will be out bike riding or something with his friends, and we can postpone the showdown.

As they walked into the backyard, it did seem as if his wish was coming true. The only person out in the yard was Mr. Marcus, and when they explained why they had come, he gestured towards a pile of branches in the back of the yard.

"You can help yourself to any of those," he said. "I have them all tied up in bundles already. You'll probably need two." He looked at Yitzi quizzically. "You look about my son Yoni's age. Are you in his class at school?"

"As a matter of fact, I am," Yitzi answered stiffly. He bent over the *s'chach* and heaved it onto the wagon. But Mr. Marcus was still looking at him.

118

TRAINING A PORCUPINE

"You must be new in town. Where do you live?"

"We live out on Woodcrest Avenue, next door to Mr. Davis," Yitzi answered, hoping that would be it.

But Mr. Marcus wasn't finished yet. "All the boys are out riding bikes, you know. Why didn't you join them?"

Oh, no! Yitzi groaned inwardly. He recognized that *mitzvah* gleam in Mr. Marcus's eye. He could just imagine the speech that Yoni would get when he got home. "Why didn't you invite the new boy to come along with you?" And Yoni would surely explain. The sooner he got away from here the better. But Mr. Marcus was still waiting for an answer.

"I was busy building our *sukkah* today, so I didn't have time," Yitzi answered finally, avoiding Mr. Marcus's gaze.

"You're building it?" Mr. Marcus's voice rose a notch.

Yitzi wished fervently that people wouldn't be so nosy. "Well, actually our neighbor Mr. Davis is helping me," he answered, without elaborating.

"That is really something, young man," Mr. Marcus said, sounding genuinely impressed. "I bet Yoni would love to hear about this when he gets back." Mr. Marcus glanced at his watch. "Okay. I'll be in the garage if you need me."

Hurry, hurry, Yitzi told himself as he struggled to load the branches onto his wagon. The last thing he wanted was to make two trips. He quickly piled the two bundles on top of each other, but as he was frantically tying them on, he heard the bicycles turning into the driveway. He looked

119

STEPPING STONES

up just in time to hear Yoni say, "Well, if it isn't the old Porcupine himself, picking up some quills from our pine trees." Yoni guffawed loudly at his own joke.

Yitzi wished he could be anywhere else in the world but right there. All his plans to be easy-going and friendly dissolved instantly. Forget about taming his porcupine self. He just wanted to get out of there—and fast!

Before he had a chance to move, however, Mr. Marcus stepped out of the garage. He obviously hadn't heard his son's witticism. "Did you boys hear what your friend here is doing?" he asked.

Yitzi winced at the word friend as he bent over the knots and pretended to be tightening them. He hoped against hope that Yoni hadn't noticed his father use that term.

"While you boys were out enjoying yourselves at the park," Mr. Marcus said admiringly, patting Yitzi on the back, "this young man has been building his own *sukkah*, with just old Mr. Davis helping him."

Yitzi wished fervently that the ground would open up underneath him. He knew Mr. Marcus was just trying to make him feel comfortable, but he could just imagine the cracks the boys would come up with now. Something along the lines of his using pine quills for nails, he was sure.

But he had underestimated Mr. Davis's fame. "Mr. Davis?" Yoni squealed. "Mr. Davis is helping you? How did you ever get him to even look at you, let alone help you? Everyone knows Mr. Davis can't stand the sight of anyone under the age of twenty-one!"

TRAINING A PORCUPINE

Yitzi was just about to shrug his shoulders and make his exit, when a thought suddenly struck him like a thunderbolt. Here was his chance. It was now or never!

He put his hand on the bundles of s'chach and looked straight at Yoni. "I guess it takes one porcupine to understand another," he said.

For a second there was silence. Then Yoni gave a hoot of laughter. In a minute, David, who had been Yoni's biking companion, joined in, and both of them were soon rolling around on the grass and laughing. Yitzi just stood there and grinned.

"Wow!" David wheezed finally when he had gotten his breath. "So there is a sense of humor behind the quills, huh?"

Yitzi just smiled back at him. Then he gathered up his courage and said, "Do you guys want to come back with me and see how it's turning out?"

"Sure," Yoni said, hopping onto his bike. "The *sukkah* that the porcupine built!" But he was smiling at Yitzi as he said it, and somehow the sting seemed to have gone out of the word.

Mr. Marcus smiled down at both of them. "I seem to have missed the joke, boys. But, Yitzi, if you can teach my son something about *sukkah* building, I will be delighted."

Yitzi's heart sang as he pulled his wagon back home, with Yael perched on top of the s'chach like a bright little butterfly. Yoni and David pushed their bikes slowly alongside him and fired questions at him about how he had gotten Mr. Davis to agree and about how he knew enough

121

STEPPING STONES

about woodwork to build a *sukkah*.

Yitzi couldn't believe how easy it had been. Of course, he and the other boys weren't completely comfortable together yet, but the ice had been broken. Yitzi had a funny feeling that things would only get better.

It was the first night of *Sukkos*. Yitzi looked around the crowded table and smiled. He still couldn't believe how much his world had changed in the past few days. The bubble of happiness inside him was so big that he was sure he must look fatter.

After Yoni and David had inspected the *sukkah* that day last week, David had to go home. But Yoni had stayed, and they had put the *s'chach* on together. Then they had gotten into a great game of handball that lasted so long that Mrs. Marcus had finally called up to find out where her son was. She and Mrs. Kurtner wound up talking on the phone for about an hour, ending with Mrs. Kurtner's inviting Yoni, his parents and his three little brothers for the first night of *Sukkos*.

So the little *sukkah* was bursting at the seams. Mr. Davis sat resplendent in his *tish bekeshe*, his unruly hair all slicked down for the occasion, smiling benevolently at everyone from his seat of honor at one end of the table. Yoni, all spruced up in his *Yom Tov* suit, sat between his parents across the table from Yitzi. Yael, perky and fresh, bounced excitedly in her chair next to her mother. And Mr. Kurtner, looking relaxed and happy, almost like his old self, sat at the head of the table.

TRAINING A PORCUPINE

Mr. Kurtner smiled at his son as he looked around the *sukkah*. "Before we start tonight," he said, "I would just like to thank my children for an important lesson I relearned tonight. Sitting in a *sukkah* is supposed to remind us that Hashem is really in charge, that our spacious safe homes are not really our security." Mr. Kurtner paused for a moment. "As some of you may know, this *sukkah* almost didn't get built. I was so busy with my job that I forgot the important lesson of *Sukkos*—that I have to do what I am supposed to do and Hashem will take care of the rest. It took Yitzi and Yael to remind me of this and I want to thank them."

Mr. Davis harumphed loudly from the end of the table. "I also learned an important lesson from the *sukkah* building," he said. "I always used to think that young folks nowadays were a bunch of . . . a bunch of . . ." For a minute the old grouchy Mr. Davis was visible again from under his grizzly eyebrows. "Well, never mind what I thought. Your youngsters turned out to be fine young workers, really fine."

"Yes," Mr. Kurtner said. "After a talk I had with Yitzi tonight, I find that a lot of people learned some important lessons from this *sukkah*."

A pine needle from the *schach* floated down and landed on the table in front of Yitzi. He looked across the table, caught Yoni's eye and winked as they all pushed back their chairs to stand up for *Kiddush*.

A Sparrow's Song

A Sparrow's Song

TZILA RUSHED INTO HER ROOM AND CLOSED THE DOOR, resisting the urge to slam it. She sat down on her bed with a thump and picked up her pillow, squeezing it with all her might.

"So what!" she muttered fiercely to herself. "So what if the faucet dripped all night? So how much was wasted anyway? A half a cup?"

Grandma was slowly driving her crazy. She was sure of it. If she was still sane by the end of this six-week stay, it would be a miracle. No doubt about it.

When her parents had told her that they would be going to Israel for six weeks because of Abba's job and that

STEPPING STONES

she would have to stay with Grandma, she had known that it would be difficult. But she had never dreamed it would be this bad.

Tzila had never gotten along with Grandma. Ever since she could remember, Grandma's visits to her parents had been punctuated by their spats. Whether it was about the type of clothes she wore, the time she "wasted" on the phone talking to friends or her lack of kitchen skills, Grandma always seemed to find something wrong with Tzila. The visits always ended with Tzila tearful and insulted and her grandmother indignant and disappointed.

It wasn't that her grandmother was mean to her or meant to insult her. She just couldn't see any value in a girl who sat around and read all day and didn't know how to knit stockings with her eyes closed, like Grandma claimed she could do when she was that age. That complaint had always struck Tzila as too funny to be insulting. Even if she ever did learn to knit stockings, with or without her eyes closed, she couldn't imagine what she would do with them once they were knit!

Tzila jumped up from her bed and began pacing the carpet in the small guest room, planting her feet firmly in the middle of each red rose. The whole situation is just so ridiculous, she fumed to herself. I told Abba and Imma that it wouldn't work, but they were so convinced that Grandma and I just needed a little time together to get to know each other. They figured that once we were better acquainted, we would both be so overwhelmed with each other's virtues that we would be the best of friends.

A SPARROW'S SONG

Tzila snorted at her reflection in the mirror. How can we possibly be friends when we don't agree on a single issue? How can I be understanding of her when not one thing that woman does makes any sense to me? Grandma is so concerned with things, she forgets all about people! She is so determined not to let things go to waste that she forgets about other people's feelings. She picked up her brush from the dresser and threw it down again.

The memory of that afternoon's scene rose up in her mind again, making her scowl so fiercely that for a moment she was startled by her reflection in the mirror.

She had been sitting there peacefully, looking out the window, enjoying the way the branches of the rosebush outside her grandmother's window looked so stark and black against the white snow. She was imagining the poem she would write about it in her mind. Suddenly, she was catapulted out of her reverie by Grandma storming into the room and flicking the curtains closed right in front of her very nose.

"Don't you see that the sun is shining on the furniture, Tzila?" Grandma had demanded, glaring up at Tzila from her full height of five feet two inches and managing somehow to look tall. "My furniture is still unfaded after thirty-six years, because I make sure to keep the sun out of this room. Why don't you use your head, Tzila?"

Tzila bit her tongue, heroically not replying. Inside, though, she was fuming. She wished she could have said, "I am using my head, Grandma! My head tells me that I would rather have faded furniture and sun-filled rooms

STEPPING STONES

than thirty-six-year-old furniture that looked new, if it meant the sun couldn't come in!"

Before she had a chance to think of how to word her reply more respectfully, Grandma continued her tirade. "And another thing, Tzila, you left the faucet dripping in the bathroom again last night. I have a good mind to start charging you for the wasted water!" Grandma twitched a dust cover over the arm chair impatiently. "I'm sure you know that people are starving in this world. How can you waste water? And the number of paper towels I found in the garbage this morning... In my days, we used a *shmatte* to wipe down the counter tops, not all this disposable stuff ... But I guess it's no use talking to you about it. You young people all think that money grows on trees." And with a last venomous glance from her piercing blue eyes, Grandma had stormed out of the room, leaving Tzila gazing after her, helpless with rage.

Now in the privacy of her own room, Tzila silently gave vent to all her angry feelings. And will it help the starving people if I use a *shmatte* to clean the counters instead of paper towels? It never bothered Imma ... She was just proud of me for wiping down the counters. Tzila stopped pacing and sat down on her bed resignedly. What could you expect from a woman who saves the water in which she boils her eggs to water the plants, and washes the floor with water she used to do the laundry by hand (to save wear and tear on the washing machine)? You would think she was a pauper the way she scrimps and saves! We'll just never see eye to eye! And I'm stuck here with her

A SPARROW'S SONG

for the next five weeks, like it or not!

"Tzila," Grandma's voice wafted up from downstairs, "I need your help peeling some potatoes."

So Grandma hadn't given up on her after all. Tzila cast a longing glance at the book on her bedside table and turned to go. Grandma was still going to continue her campaign to turn Tzila into a *balebuste*, come what may. In her usual practical, determined, unemotional way, she probably hadn't even realized she had hurt Tzila's feelings.

"I hope Imma is proud of me—wherever she is over there in Israel. I'm certainly doing my best." And groaning inwardly, Tzila marched resolutely downstairs to peel potatoes.

When Tzila woke up the next morning, the sun was streaming in through the window. She had surreptitiously left the curtains open the night before. A solitary sparrow, who for some reason had decided to brave New York in the winter, was chirping at her from his perch on the rosebush outside. Tzila immediately felt better herself. Somehow, she had the feeling that she and Grandma would work things out. After all, they had to live together for the next five weeks, and they couldn't actually spend it at each other's throats!

Tzila reached for the phone on her bedside table, one of Grandma's concessions to her "spoiled granddaughter." She hoped she would still be able to catch Dalya before she went down for breakfast. She was sure Dalya had been up for hours already. Dalya was like Grandma

131

STEPPING STONES

in that respect. She was the sensible-early-to-bed-and-early-to-rise type.

"Good morning, Dalya," Tzila said, making sure to keep her voice low. Grandma would think it was the epitome of laziness and sloth to talk on the phone in bed before getting up.

"Hi, Tzila!" Dalya sounded as chipper as always. "How is it going? Are you still planning to run away or has this bright morning changed your mind?"

Tzila lay back on her pillow and smiled into the receiver. It was amazing how Dalya always knew what she was feeling.

"Nope," she said, "I've decided to try and stick it out. My plan is to be so sweet and helpful today when I come home from school that Grandma won't even be able to remember what happened when I peeled her potatoes yesterday."

Dalya giggled. "What happened? Did you try and use a fork instead of a peeler?"

"No, it was just that the peels came off in little spurts all over the kitchen table and floor and me. Grandma very subtly mentioned how she and her sister used to have contests with each other to see if they could get all the peels off in one long, neat swirl. She made sure I realized that in those days they didn't have peelers, either. It was all done with a sharp knife."

Dalya sighed in sympathy. "It's hopeless, Tzila. She will never make a *balebuste* out of you! But did you tell her you were chosen to write the play for our *Rosh Chodesh*

A SPARROW'S SONG

assembly? That is pretty impressive, isn't it?"

Tzila snorted in derision. "Depends to whom. Now if I had been chosen to cook for the assembly . . . that might have impressed her."

Dalya's laugh bubbled over the wire. "You cooking, Tzila! You are my best friend and all, but I think I would rather eat peanut butter sandwiches."

"Excuse me!" Tzila said, pretending to be insulted. "I'll have you know that my scrambled eggs are a real delicacy, as long as I don't forget that they are on the fire and let them burn."

"Well," Dalya said in a commiserating tone, "your parents will be back before you know it, and at least *they* appreciate you."

It was true, although Tzila could never understand it. Imma was Grandma's daughter, but Tzila's creativity was Imma's pride and joy. She was constantly encouraging Tzila to write, and she was Tzila's most enthusiastic fan.

"Yes, Imma will be delighted to hear that I'm writing the play. I'll have to write her about it." Tzila sat up and scrambled for her fuzzy pink slippers. "I'd better get up and get moving. You are probably all dressed and ready for school already," she said accusingly.

"I am all ready, Tzila, and you better hurry up, too. I'm not going to wait for you for twenty minutes again! And your grandmother is probably wondering why you haven't come down yet. Where is she right now?"

"Oh, she is bustling around the kitchen, getting ready

STEPPING STONES

to leave for her *chessed* project." Tzila glanced at her clock on the bedside table. She really had better get moving herself.

"You really have to hand it to her," Dalya said. "She sure manages to pack a lot of *chessed* in. Where is she going today?"

"It's Tuesday, so she is probably going to the orphanage to make lunch. No, maybe it is her day to feed that old lady in the old age home. Or maybe she is going to the hospital to deliver mail. Well, I don't know, but it is one of those."

"It's interesting." Dalya's voice had taken on a contemplative note. "Both she and your mother are so busy helping people out, but they do it so differently."

"Yeah," Tzila agreed, stretching the coils of the wire to reach her clothes. "But Imma's type of *chessed* is much more my style."

"What do you mean?" Dalya asked.

"Oh, you know, I would rather be a psychologist like Imma and counsel a kid in an orphanage, than sit there in a greasy lunchroom making a lunch no one enjoys."

In her mind's eye, Tzila could picture herself walking down the hall of an orphanage with a small girl who looked up at her trustingly with big round eyes. She could just imagine reaching out with her words and touching that little girl's broken heart.

Dalya's practical voice broke into her reverie. "Well, someone has got to make the lunches, you know. Understanding people and being sensitive is all very nice, but

A SPARROW'S SONG

this world wouldn't work very well without people who are not afraid to roll up their sleeves and get their hands dirty."

Tzila, who knew that Dalya leaned towards the more practical side of life and loved cooking and knitting, smiled to herself. "You're right, Dalya. But speaking of being practical, if I am going to implement my plan of being a ray of helpfulness in Grandma's life, then I better get going. Grandma will not appreciate it if I am late to breakfast again!"

Tzila spent the day in school, alternating between planning the *Rosh Chodesh* play and picturing herself being a shining star of helpfulness to Grandma that evening. Maybe she would peel all the vegetables and have a delicious soup ready for supper before Grandma came home that night. Dalya would tell her how.

When Tzila finally opened the door of the house that evening, she was delighted to see that Grandma wasn't back yet, and she hurried into the kitchen to begin peeling.

The open window caught her eye, and she rested her elbows on the sill for a moment. She decided to take a few minutes to look out the window and plot the last scene of the play before she started. From Dalya's instructions, it didn't sound like the soup would take too long.

It was three quarters of an hour later when the scuffle of Grandma's work shoes in the kitchen snapped Tzila out of her reverie.

In one quick glance, Grandma took in the pile of vegetables on the table, the clock on the wall and her

STEPPING STONES

granddaughter's stance at the window.

"Tzila!" she wailed. "Didn't my daughter teach you anything? You've been home for three quarters of an hour already! I especially left the vegetables out on the table hoping you would take the hint and make some soup. And you have just been sitting there daydreaming! Killing time!"

Tzila jumped to her feet guiltily. Grandma made it sound as if Tzila had murdered someone. How had this happened? She had wanted so much to make Grandma happy with her this evening, and now this! How could she ever explain herself?

But Tzila had underestimated Grandma's kind heart. Seeing her granddaughter's stricken face, she took a step forward and patted Tzila on the shoulder. "It's okay, dear. I know you didn't mean it. It's just the idea of sitting at the window for forty-five minutes. My mother used to say, `Better to unravel a perfectly good sweater and re-knit it than to sit with idle hands.'"

Tzila managed a half smile. Her mind was whirling. What an inordinate waste of time to re-knit a perfectly good sweater when during that same time you could be looking out the window, enjoying Hashem's beautiful world and plotting a play that everyone would enjoy.

Forget it, she thought. We will just never understand each other. Not unless I became a different person overnight. It was true that the things Grandma was involved in were important and kept the world running, as Dalya had said. But she would still rather be sensitive, intuitive,

A SPARROW'S SONG

caring, and use her head instead of her hands.

Mechanically, she picked up a potato and the peeler. "I'm sorry, Grandma," she said, "Let me help you peel them now." Maybe later she would tell Grandma about Dalya's vegetable soup recipe and how she had planned to make it for her. Although she didn't suppose it would make much difference. Grandma would probably just say something about good intentions not being very productive.

Tzila wasn't sure which woke her the next morning, the oppressive gray sky and her friendly sparrow's absence on the rosebush outside, or the quiet in the house. She lay still for a moment trying to figure out what was different. A quick glance at her bedside clock reassured her that she hadn't overslept. It was seven-thirty, the same time she got up every morning.

She strained her ears for a minute. Where was Grandma? That was what was so different. Usually, by the time Tzila stumbled out of bed, Grandma was already up for hours. Tzila could always hear her bustling around in the kitchen, banging pots and silverware around or talking on the phone with Mrs. Perlmutter, who had insomnia and always enjoyed an early morning call. But this morning, the house was silent, with the muffled tick of the alarm clock sounding ominously louder than usual. Could it be that her clock was slow and that Grandma had already left for the day? Tzila jammed her feet into her pink slippers and grabbed her robe. A sense of foreboding gripped her throat as she hurried downstairs, and a glance

STEPPING STONES

at the big grandfather clock in the dining room confirmed her fears. It was only seven-thirty. Where was Grandma?

"Grandma!" she called as she hurried down the long carpeted hallway. "Grandma, where are you?"

Tzila's mouth felt dry and her palms sweaty. She could feel her heart beating all the way up in her throat. She hesitated before she pushed open the swinging kitchen door. Stop being so dramatic, she told herself. Grandma is probably *davening* and that is why she is not answering. With a determined push, she swung the door open.

Grandma was lying on her back on the floor, her face gray and strange looking, her eyes closed, her *tichel* askew. Tzila put a hand over her mouth to stifle a scream and took a step backward. What had happened? Imma had told her that Grandma had a weak heart. Had Tzila caused this by being so difficult and contrary?

She took a deep breath. Quick! Quick! Think practically! What had Imma said she should do in an emergency? Call Hatzalah. That was their phone number on the wall above the phone. Tzila dialed quickly, willing her fingers to move. Next, call Uncle Dov. Her voice sounded strange and thin to her ears as she gave Aunt Rachel the details. Hanging up the phone, she bent over Grandma and felt her hands. They were still warm, and Grandma was breathing softly. What had happened? Was this what a heart attack was like?

Tzila knelt down beside Grandma and loosened her collar. She couldn't believe how little and fragile her grandmother looked. Was this the same woman around

A SPARROW'S SONG

whom she had always been so nervous? Tzila took a wet rag and wiped Grandma's forehead. She wished she knew if she was doing the right thing. Where was Hatzalah already? Tzila rushed back and forth from the window of the kitchen to Grandma's side, like a moth batting its wings against a light bulb, willing Hatzalah or Uncle Dov to come.

What if Grandma stopped breathing suddenly? Her skin looked so gray. Tzila wished she had listened more carefully at the first aid course that was offered at school. She ran back to Grandma's side and felt her pulse. It seemed to be beating normally, but Grandma's face looked so different, almost like it belonged to some anonymous stranger on the street.

The sound of a siren reached her ears, and Tzila raced to open the front door for the three big bearded men who were standing there. Two of them went straight to work on Grandma, while the third, a fatherly looking man with light blue eyes, questioned her about what happened.

Tzila answered shakily, clutching her blue robe tightly around her and feeling foolish in her fuzzy pink slippers.

Just as the Hatzalah men were lifting Grandma into the ambulance, Uncle Dov came bursting through the door like a whirlwind, his shirt half buttoned and his *yarmulka* askew. He grabbed Grandma's medical documents from the desk drawer and flew out the front door, calling to Tzila that Aunt Rachel would be over soon and that they should stay close to the phone.

Tzila closed the front door shakily and went to sit on

the couch near the big front window. She tucked her feet up under her and leaned back against the couch, trying to breathe deeply. Her feet felt like cotton wool, and her stomach was doing flip-flops.

Thoughts whirled through her head like cannonballs. Was this all her fault? Had the pressure of having an undisciplined granddaughter around the house been too much for her grandmother? Her grandmother had looked so little and vulnerable, like a little gray sparrow that Tzila had once seen lying on the snow, its tiny hooked feet up in the air.

Even after Aunt Rachel came, comforting and warm in her efficient way, Tzila still felt numb. When Uncle Dov called from the hospital to say that it was just a very slight stroke and that Grandma would probably be back home in a week, Tzila sat on the couch, still feeling empty.

It had all been a big mistake. She should never have stayed here. It was too much for Grandma. And besides, Imma had been all wrong. There was nothing she could learn from Grandma. Grandma might be a wonderful person who did lots of *mitzvos*, but they just were not the kind of *mitzvos* Tzila was interested in emulating.

When Uncle Dov came home from the hospital a few hours later, he suggested that she call her parents in Israel so that her mother could decide if she wanted to come back. Tzila almost wept in relief. She would be able to go back home again. Her mother would stay here to take care of Grandma, and she would be able to pretend that the whole two weeks had never happened.

A SPARROW'S SONG

By the time Tzila fell asleep that night, she felt a little better. This, of course, was only after having Uncle Dov and Aunt Rachel reassure her that Grandma's stroke had had nothing to do with her, and after hearing her mother's decision to come back early. She was glad she had convinced Uncle Dov and Aunt Rachel to let her sleep alone at Grandma's house. It was nice to have the whole house to herself and not to have to make conversation with and be polite to her aunt and uncle after her harrowing day.

The sharp peal of the telephone the next morning startled Tzila out of a deep sleep. She shook her head groggily and fumbled for the phone. Goodness, it was only seven o'clock! Who could be calling this early?

The voice at the other end was vaguely familiar, though it took a few minutes for Tzila's sleep-befuddled brain to identify it.

"Oh, oh, this must be the granddaughter. Oh dear! Oh dear! Such terrible news ! Oh dear! And we will all suffer as well! I tell you, granddaughter dear, such a woman as your grandmother you don't find every day! No, not at all, not at all. Not even once a year, and now high and dry we are left. Yes, high and dry, I tell you!"

Tzila grinned into the receiver. She knew who this was! It must be Mrs. Kramer from the orphanage. Tzila remembered that fluttery voice and the disjointed sentences from when her grandmother had introduced her to Mrs. Kramer in *shul*.

"Good morning, Mrs. Kramer, and how are you?" Tzila broke in.

STEPPING STONES

"Oh, *a gutte, a gutte,* so polite. Oh yes, she remembers my name, yes, yes. But today for lunch what will we do? And the poor grandmother sick in the hospital . . . Who could know? Oh my! Oh my!" The fluttery voice sounded like it was going to cry.

"You are worried about who will make lunch today in the orphanage, Mrs. Kramer?" Tzila asked, feeling as if she were deciphering a code.

"Oh yes, oh yes. Can't ask granddaughter . . . but who else . . . who else? Poor children be hungry. The last minute . . . who could know? Who could know? Oh dear, poor grandmother in hospital . . ."

Tzila felt like she was being blown by a wind. The lady obviously wanted her to volunteer to come and make lunch instead of her grandmother. For a moment, Tzila hesitated while the fluttery voice at the other end of the line continued lamenting in her ear. Somehow, the word orphanage held such an attraction for her. All those poor, lonely children, and she, with her gentle, compassionate ear, could give them hope.

Don't be ridiculous, she told herself. You will be stuck there in that greasy kitchen for hours. You probably won't even see any of the children. She thought for a minute. Maybe she should do it anyway. This lady really sounded desperate, although Tzila suspected that she always sounded as if all of life was one big crisis. Well, why not? Uncle Dov had said she should stay home from school today anyway, after yesterday's shock, and she had nothing in particular to do at home.

A SPARROW'S SONG

The voice in her ear was still going on. "Such a tragedy. Whom to ask? Lunch for the children... The granddaughter busy probably . . . grandmother in hospital . . . oh dear . . . oh dear . . ."

Tzila took a deep breath. "Okay, Mrs. Kramer, I'll come instead of my grandmother today. What time do you want me?"

"Oh! Like grandmother, like granddaughter . . . such *a gutte . . . a gutte . . .* Yes. Yes, ten-thirty would be fine. Oh, such *nachas* for the grandmother . . . poor children will be hungry . . . *a gutte . . . a gutte.*" The fluttery voice threatened to break into tears again out of sheer gratitude.

Tzila took advantage of the break in conversation. "Okay, Mrs. Kramer, I'll be there at ten-thirty," she said and hung up the phone with a feeling of relief.

But later that morning, when Tzila was bustled into the big kitchen by the big, buxom Mrs. Kramer, whose girth belied her high fluttery voice, she wondered whether she hadn't gotten herself into more than she had bargained for.

The smell of greasy chicken hovered in the air. The shabby, unpainted walls and chipped formica counters didn't make for a very cheerful atmosphere.

Mrs. Kramer bustled her over to a counter where a huge vat of potatoes stood waiting.

"These peel, make mashed potatoes . . . poor children for lunch . . . grandmother good cook . . . now make do . . . make do . . . peel quickly . . . must quick cook . . . poor children for lunch." And Mrs. Kramer bustled away to

STEPPING STONES

supervise another volunteer who was cutting up pieces of chicken with a huge butcher knife, splattering bits of feathers and fat all over the counter.

Tzila stifled a small grin and a sigh of relief. At least she knew how to peel potatoes, even if the peels didn't come off in neat swirls.

An hour and a half later, Tzila didn't feel so confident. The vat of potatoes to be peeled was still a quarter full. Her fingers and hands ached and so did her legs from standing in one position for so long.

Three other ladies, who also must have been volunteers, had come over to tell her how much they missed her grandmother and how she always lightened up the atmosphere with her stories and jokes. They all mentioned how quickly her grandmother would work, and how the potato peels just disappeared under her hands.

Tzila's lips were dry and cracked from the potato peel dust. She was sure, from Mrs. Kramer's anxious glances in her direction, that no one had ever taken longer to peel a vat of potatoes in the orphanage's history. She could think of nothing she would like to do less than tell stories and jokes. Tzila sank lower and lower into her shoes with each anecdote told by the other volunteers.

Tzila's spirits lifted a little once the potatoes were finally finished and cooked. Mrs. Kramer directed her to the assembly line in front of the window, where her job would be to distribute the mashed potatoes to the children. If she didn't perform as well as her grandmother in potato peeling, at least she was sure Mrs. Kramer and all

A SPARROW'S SONG

the other ladies would be impressed with her kind and caring manner with the orphans. After all, that's what's important in life. People!

The sudden onslaught of girls descending into the lunchroom changed her mind very quickly. These girls seemed like perfectly normal, happy, cheerful, chattering kids who were much more interested in the amount of mashed potatoes she put on their plates than in the care and concern in her smile. Her smile became a little tarnished as the afternoon wore on and the twenty-third broken-hearted orphan came to complain about the potato peels in the mashed potatoes. No one seemed particularly interested in her understanding responses, and some of their remarks were downright insulting.

It didn't help any when Mrs. Sidell, the chicken cutting volunteer, murmured into her ear about how her grandmother managed these children so well and how she had them all hanging around after lunch just to chat with her.

During the whole raucous, exhausting, noisy afternoon, Tzila only managed to have one meaningful conversation. A ten-year-old girl came down after the others had left and applied a soothing salve to Tzila's wounded ego by telling her that the potatoes were delicious and that she hoped that when she grew up she would look just like Tzila. But when she added that Tzila's smile reminded her of Tzila's grandmother, Tzila could only wonder if all these people were really talking about the same strict, critical, insensitive grandmother she thought she knew so well.

STEPPING STONES

As she dragged her weary body onto the bus that afternoon, the only compensating thought she could think of was that Grandma certainly couldn't write a play for the *Rosh Chodesh* assembly, even if she could handle a bunch of wild little girls. But it was a hollow comfort, and she knew it.

Tzila woke up the next morning determined to put the whole episode at the orphanage out of her mind. After all, she reasoned, she had never aspired to be a kitchen volunteer, and her not having done as good a job as her grandmother made no difference in the long run.

And it wasn't like she had nothing to think about. In fact, she was tingling with anticipation. Only two more days and her parents would be back. Uncle Dov kept saying what a pity it was that they had to cut their visit short when Grandma was really fine and would be home by the end of the week. He had tried, via the telephone, to convince Tzila's mother that it wasn't necessary to come back. He had tried to persuade her that it was only three more weeks and that Grandma could manage fine with Tzila to take care of her until then.

But Tzila's mother refused to be dissuaded. Tzila wondered if it wasn't because her mother sensed how unhappy Tzila was. Still, the thought of going back to her own comfortable home with Abba (she was sure her mother would want to stay with Grandma for a while) made her feelings of guilt fade comfortably away. She could just imagine not having to worry about wasting water, daydreaming, admiring the sunset and being lec-

146

A SPARROW'S SONG

tured on the unlikelihood of her becoming a *balebuste*.

Tzila did a little skip around the bedroom as she dressed, glad that Grandma wasn't down in the kitchen to tell her she sounded like a baby elephant. The ring of the telephone startled her in midskip, and she dashed across the bedroom to get it, hoping it was Abba and Imma calling to tell her the time of their arrival.

But it wasn't. It was Mrs. Gold, from the old age home, stern, crisp and to the point, who wanted to know if she could come and feed her grandmother's old lady during her lunch break from school that day. It was amazing how the news of her grandmother's illness seemed to have spread so quickly through the *chessed* organizations.

Mrs. Gold, though not given to fluttering, made it quite clear to Tzila that her grandmother was a priceless find and that the whole old age home held her in awe. In fact, Tzila was uncomfortably aware that Mrs. Gold was quite sure that Tzila couldn't compare.

But not even Mrs. Gold's suspicions could puncture her happiness balloon that day, and full of good will, Tzila happily agreed to come at twelve o'clock.

All through the morning, Tzila daydreamed to herself about the old age home. She remembered a story she had once written (and gotten an "A" on) about a poor, lonely old lady in an old age home and how a young girl who used to come visit her every week brightened up her life.

Who knows? This lady might love Tzila so much that she would ask Mrs. Gold if Tzila could take her grandmother's place! Everyone would be so impressed

STEPPING STONES

with her sensitivity, that a young girl of her age could relate so well to an old woman.

Indeed, as Tzila walked through the halls of the old age home on the way to Mrs. Gold's office that afternoon, smiling and nodding at the women sitting around in their wheelchairs, it did seem as if her daydreams were materializing. The old ladies seemed delighted by her presence, and a few even stopped her, asked questions and were happy to hear news of her grandmother.

Mrs. Gold looked up from her desk and smiled frostily in greeting. "Good morning, dear. I am glad you are on time. Mrs. Hale doesn't like to be kept waiting. I'll walk you down to her room and show you what has to be done."

Somehow, Mrs. Gold's calm, capable air, trim blue suit and beautifully styled wig made Tzila feel rumpled and inadequate. As she followed Mrs. Gold's click clacking heels down the long hall, she began to wonder if she hadn't made a mistake in agreeing to come.

Mrs. Gold paused outside the door of Mrs. Hale's room and gave Tzila an appraising glance. At Tzila's nod, she swung the door open and stepped into the room. Tzila followed and immediately recoiled with horror. Mrs. Hale was lying back on her pillow, her wispy gray hair sticking out in tufts from under her kerchief. Her head was back, and saliva dripped out of the side of her mouth. From what Tzila could see, she didn't seem to have any teeth, and her thin, fragile fingers picked fitfully at her blanket.

"Good morning, Mrs. Hale," Mrs. Gold said cheerfully, and Tzila managed to echo her quietly.

A SPARROW'S SONG

It didn't seem to make much difference, because Mrs. Hale didn't acknowledge either of their greetings. She just continued lying there, her eyes staring blankly at the ceiling, her breath coming raspily.

Mrs. Gold bustled busily around the room, cranking up the side of Mrs. Hale's bed and fluffing her pillows so that she was more or less in a sitting position.

Tzila stood frozen to the spot, watching her and dreading the moment she would leave. This was awful! How could she stand to be in the same room with this poor person for half an hour, let alone touch her and feed her? What was she going to do? How did her grandmother do this every week?

Mrs. Gold was talking all the while, telling Mrs. Hale about the weather and explaining to Tzila where Mrs. Hale was from, but Tzila could barely concentrate. Wasn't there some way she could get out of this? Mrs. Gold wheeled the tray of food closer to the bed and indicated a chair to Tzila.

"Here we go, Tzila. First settle yourself down right over here. I think Mrs. Hale enjoys the applesauce the most, so you can start with that."

Tzila opened her mouth to reply, protest, beg for help—she didn't know what. "No, please don't leave me here," she wanted to yell. "I can't do it." But Mrs. Gold was already at the door.

Tzila stared numbly at Mrs. Hale. There was just no way that she could do this. She was sure her stomach just wouldn't stand for it. She stepped forward gingerly and took the spoon in her hand. At that moment, Mrs. Hale's head lolled to the side and saliva began to dribble down her cheek onto the pillow. Her toothless gums glistened and her tongue rolled halfway out. Tzila gripped the spoon more tightly and tried to control the wave of nausea that threatened to engulf her. She just couldn't do this. She tried to avert her gaze as she directed the spoon in the general direction of Mrs. Hale's mouth, when suddenly Mrs. Hale coughed. Applesauce and saliva splattered all over the bedclothes, the tray and Tzila's hand.

Tzila jumped up from the chair where she had been sitting as if she had been stung. If she didn't get out of here fast, she was sure she would be sick herself.

She half walked, half ran down the hall to Mrs. Gold's office. Her heart was pounding, her stomach rolling. Mrs. Gold looked up, startled at Tzila's abrupt entrance.

"Is everything okay, Tzila?" she asked, standing up quickly.

Tzila gulped hard. She didn't even care anymore what Mrs. Gold thought of her. She just knew she had to get out of there fast. "Mrs. Hale is fine, but I'm very sorry. I am just not feeling well. I . . . I . . . won't be able to feed her lunch. Maybe you can get someone else?"

Tzila grabbed her pocketbook and backed hurriedly towards the door. She was terrified that Mrs. Gold would protest or call her back, and she didn't want to stay to give her a chance to do so.

Tzila was already halfway down the hall when she heard Mrs. Gold saying, "Well, I hope you feel better, dear, but you have really left us in a pickle. I don't know what I'll do now!"

Tzila pushed the big door of the old age home open and gulped in the cool, clear, fresh air. Don't worry, she told herself as she hurried along. I'm sure she will find someone else to feed Mrs. Hale.

She glanced at her watch as she turned into the schoolyard. Good, there were twenty minutes left to lunch, so hopefully she would still have a chance to pour her heart out to Dalya before class started. She felt in desperate need of some sympathy.

Dalya's reaction, though, was a little disappointing. She sat cross-legged under the big oak tree in the front yard of the school and looked up at Tzila, who was perched on the low stone wall next to her.

"Well, at whom are you so angry?" she asked quietly.

Tzila crumpled up her brown paper bag. She hadn't been able to eat her lunch at all. "Well, isn't it obvious? How could Mrs. Gold have given me such a difficult patient? I mean she knows I am just a young girl in high school. I am happy to help out, but that is a job for an older woman!"

"Do you really think so?" Dalya's gaze was direct. "What makes you think that when you are older you will be any different? I mean, you seem to be very sensitive and caring right now. Why shouldn't you have been able to handle this right now, and if not now, why should it be any different when you are older?"

Tzila pulled a twig from a branch and crumpled it

STEPPING STONES

between her fingers. Sometimes Dalya could be so annoying! As much as she appreciated her clear head and logical way of thinking, sometimes she could really be dense!

"Come on, Dalya!" she snapped. "Of course, it will be different. Older people aren't so squeamish. I mean, Grandma does it every week, and it doesn't bother her a bit!"

Dalya leaned back on her hands. "Well, do you think that it is just because she is older? Maybe it has to do with her personality. Maybe, with all your sensitivity, you won't ever be able to help that kind of person. You will just notice all the unpleasant details that your grandmother wouldn't even see."

Tzila thought for a moment. Dalya was probably right. That was typical of Grandma. If something practical needed to be done, she just plowed ahead and did it. She didn't dwell on it and think about it. She probably hadn't even noticed all the things that had so nauseated Tzila.

Tzila glanced at her watch and jumped up. It was getting late. "Well, even if that is true," she said to Dalya, "I would still rather have my personality and be able to understand and empathize with someone than be like Grandma, who is good and practical but basically insensitive."

Dalya held out her hand to Tzila. "Pull me up, will you?" She leaned down to gather up her books. "What good did it do for Mrs. Hale that you could relate to how uncomfortable and pathetic her situation was? Isn't the whole point of being sensitive to be able to help people?"

A SPARROW'S SONG

Tzila shuffled her books impatiently. Didn't Dalya understand anything? "I'm not talking about Mrs. Hale now. I'm talking about how Grandma is so insensitive to my needs and how she can't relate to me at all. Despite all her *chessed*, I felt miserable in her home, and I can't wait until my parents come back so that I can escape."

Dalya was silent on the way back to the classroom, and Tzila had the uncomfortable feeling that she wasn't convinced. It wasn't until they were settled in their seats and about to begin that Dalya turned and said to her, "I still think that sometimes it's not good to be so sensitive. I'm sure Mrs. Hale and Mrs. Gold would have appreciated it if you were just good and practical like your grandmother."

Tzila wanted to retort, but before she could think of what to say, Mrs. Klein opened her science book and began, leaving Tzila with Dalya's words to rankle her for the rest of the day.

When Tzila unlocked the door to her grandmother's house that afternoon, she smelled vegetable soup wafting from the kitchen and found Aunt Rachel bustling around, her arms piled high with clean linen.

"Hi, Tzila," Aunt Rachel greeted her as she made her way to the bedroom. "You know your grandmother is coming back tomorrow, and with your parents arriving on Tuesday, I thought I would come over and freshen things up a little. Your grandmother always worries so much about other people, I felt it was time someone worried about her."

STEPPING STONES

Why was everyone always praising Grandma? Tzila wondered to herself. It was so annoying! Didn't anyone else ever see her as she did?

She followed Aunt Rachel into the bedroom and perched herself on the edge of the armchair, as she watched Aunt Rachel neatly tucking in the corners of the fresh sheets around Grandma's mattress.

"So my parents aren't coming until Tuesday?" she asked.

"No," Aunt Rachel replied. "They called and said they couldn't get an earlier flight. I hope you won't mind. It will only be two more days alone with Grandma."

Tzila stifled a sigh. She couldn't wait to get out of this house already. Especially after that scene at the old age home.

Aunt Rachel glanced at her suddenly, with concern in her face. "What's wrong, Tzila? You look a little down, yourself. Did you have a hard day?"

Tzila managed a small smile. "I'm okay, really," she said. She wondered whether Aunt Rachel would also think she should have stayed to feed Mrs. Hale. Maybe she should ask her opinion?

Just then the doorbell rang and Aunt Rachel groaned. "Oh, I still have so much to do in here, Tzila. Will you get it? It's probably one of those *meshulachim* again."

Tzila opened the door to a short, gray-bearded man with a black briefcase and a tired look on his face. She was glad Aunt Rachel was in the house so that she could invite him in. She had hated having to turn all the other

A SPARROW'S SONG

meshulachim away, as she had since Grandma was gone.

"Please come in," she said, ushering him into the living room.

The man perched himself uncomfortably on the edge of the couch. "Mrs. Gold is in?" he asked in halting English.

"I'm sorry, my grandmother isn't here right now," Tzila said. "Maybe I can help you?"

The man's face creased into a worried half smile. "*Oy,* this is not good. Tomorrow, early, I leave for Israel, and I did want to see your grandmother before I go. She is one of our big supporters . . ."

Tzila smiled to herself. They must really be in sad shape if Grandma is one of their big supporters. Considering Grandma's stinginess to which Tzila had been subjected this whole week, she couldn't imagine that Grandma's donations could sustain anyone, let alone a whole organization.

"Well, let me ask my aunt if she can help you," Tzila said reassuringly.

She left the man ruffling worriedly through his briefcase, while she searched for Aunt Rachel.

"Ask the man to give you a receipt of Grandma's previous donation," Aunt Rachel advised from the top of the stepladder where she was busily dusting the blinds in Grandma's room. "And then check to see if it is the right amount according to the date in Grandma's *tzeddakah* ledger in her top desk drawer. Grandma asked us to write out checks in case any of her regulars came along."

Tzila was glad to have some positive news to relay

STEPPING STONES

back to the man in the living room, and she waited patiently while the man leafed through his receipts.

"Here it is," the man said triumphantly, waving the pink slip in the air. "Yes, last *Kislev* your good grandmother gave us one thousand dollars."

Tzila, who was leaning against the dining room table, almost fell over. "A thousand dollars?" she said, reaching for the paper. "Are you sure you've got the right name?"

The man nodded emphatically. "Yes, your grandmother is a very generous lady. Very generous!"

Tzila took the paper doubtfully. Well, she'd check in Grandma's ledger. There was probably some mistake. Like a double zero mistake, at least!

Tzila pulled the ledger out of the drawer and glanced quickly through the pages until she found the date listed on the receipt. She didn't want to keep the man waiting too long. Especially not for what was probably just a ten dollar donation!

Her finger ran quickly across the line. Yes, this was the date and the check number. Suddenly, Tzila's finger stopped. This was the amount column. Could she be seeing things?

Right there in black and white, in Grandma's own, clear, spiky handwriting, it said one thousand dollars. But that wasn't all. Tzila let her eye travel up and down the column. What was this? Could this really be her grandmother's book?

Yeshivas . . . $1,000
Orphanage . . . $1,200

A SPARROW'S SONG

Yeshivas . . . $2,000

Home for . . . $1,500

Scenes flitted through her head like the colors in a kaleidoscope. Grandma scraping the jar of mayonnaise out to the last speck, intoning, "A penny saved is a penny earned, my dear!"

Grandma reusing the plastic bags she got from the vegetable store and not buying new bags on principle, "The things people waste nowadays." Grandma yelling at her for leaving the light on overnight, "Money doesn't grow on trees, you know!"

Tzila stared blankly at the page in front of her, the words blurring before her eyes. So this is what Grandma was all about. This is where she spent her money. And Tzila had thought she was stingy!

A memory of how she herself had spent her last allowance came to her mind. She had felt so noble when she had given one dollar over ten percent to *tzeddakah* and had cheerfully spent the rest on a new top which she hadn't really needed.

When was the last time Grandma had bought herself anything? Tears slipped down Tzila's cheeks unheeded, making dark splotches on the neatly printed pages. She was no mathematician, but the vast sums recorded clearly exceeded ten percent of Grandma's income.

Images of Grandma peeling potatoes in the orphanage, joking and smiling all the time, and of Grandma cheerfully feeding Mrs. Hale every week, without a word about it to anyone, filled Tzila's mind.

STEPPING STONES

Maybe everybody else was right and she was wrong after all. How could she have been so blind? Her grandmother had been desperately trying to get her to see past her own little world, and she had resented every prod and nudge.

Tzila sat hunched over the ledger, her mind whirling. Why hadn't she seen what everyone else seemed to see? She wished she could talk to her grandmother right then, but a cough from the other room reminded her that the man was still waiting.

She stood up, firmly clutching the ledger, and went to her aunt to get the check. Now she knew what she had to do—no, what she wanted to do. She would call up her mother right away and try and convince her to stay out her six-week visit. She knew her mother would understand once she explained. She would tell her how she still had so much to learn from her grandmother and needed some more time. Her mother might even be relieved to be able to stay, as long as she didn't need to worry about Tzila.

She knew it wouldn't be easy. She and her grandmother were too different for things to run perfectly smooth, but Tzila was determined to try.

And as Tzila passed the window on the way back to the living room, she noticed her brave little sparrow back on its branch, chirping lustily, its beady black eyes gleaming and bright.